CH00854004

HOLY POISON

Book Five

THE HERETICS

By

Margaret Brazear

Copyright © Margaret Brazear 2015

http://www.historical-romance.com

INTRODUCTION

The period between the death of the young Protestant King Edward VI in 1547 and the death of his half-sister, Catholic Queen Mary I in 1553 was one of the most confusing and turbulent in English history.

It is well known that King Henry VIII broke with the Church of Rome and the Pope in order to divorce his wife, Katherine of Aragon, and marry Anne Boleyn. He did not, however, break with the Catholic faith, instead he merely developed his own version of it. He destroyed the monasteries and smashed the idols more to gain their riches than from any matters of conscience and for years he adhered to his version of Catholicism.

His sixth and last wife, Catherine Parr, tried to convert him to Protestant thinking but she had not totally succeeded in that when the King died. His only son, Edward, was raised by Protestant uncles and on becoming King at the tender age of only ten years, he supported those uncles in declaring Protestantism to be the religion of England.

Catholics were outlawed, the mass was outlawed, churches were plain with no statues or idols, the services were in English. This was the beginning of priests' holes in large houses, where a Catholic family would hide a priest to say mass for them, but anyone found to be Catholic would be imprisoned and their property and wealth would be confiscated.

For six years most of the country was Protestant, or pretended to be. When the King died at only fifteen years of age his half-sister, Mary took the throne, after the very brief reign of Protestant Jane Grey. A fanatical Roman Catholic, Mary swore to bring England back under the rule of the Pope and the Roman Church. Priests who had been allowed to marry under her brother's rule were forced to abandon their wives, Protestant writings and books were burned and the mass was re-introduced along with the idols which the Protestants had discarded. Once more there were relics of saints which people aid to touch, once more there was transubstantiation, the belief that the wine and bread of the Holy Communion actually became the blood and flesh of Christ, not merely a symbol of those things.

Her nickname of 'Bloody Mary' was well earned, as during her brutal campaign to return England to the Catholic church, she burned alive nearly four hundred Protestants as heretics, more than all previous monarchs put together.

Her marriage to Prince Philip II of Spain was not a popular choice, and despite two phantom pregnancies she never managed to produce an heir. On her death, her Protestant half-sister, Elizabeth, daughter of Ann Boleyn succeeded her as Queen and reigned for forty three years until 1603.

There were a few attempts by Catholics to depose Elizabeth I and replace her with Mary Queen of Scots, resulting in the Babington Plot and in Mary's eventual execution at Fotheringay Castle in Northamptonshire.

England had one more Catholic monarch, King James II, but he was ousted and the throne given to his Protestant daughter, Mary II and her husband William of Orange. Never again did a Catholic sit upon the throne of England and even today, 2015, no one in line to the throne is permitted to marry a Catholic.

The Act of Settlement 1701 precludes any Roman Catholic from the line of succession to the British throne. Neither is any member of the line allowed to marry a Roman Catholic. Prince Michael of Kent relinquished his claim to the throne on his marriage to a Roman Catholic.

Mary's zealous campaign to return England to Catholicism poisoned the people against the Church of Rome and ensured that no Catholic would ever again sit on the throne of England.

HOLY POISON tells of ordinary people who lived through those times who were forced to either change their religion or pretend to, even though it was an important part of their lives.

Many died horrible deaths by refusing to do so and this series, although fiction, is written for them – the Martyrs of the Reformation.

CHAPTER ONE

Julia sat in the bed, her pale blonde hair newly brushed and shining, her blue silk shift unfastened at the breast, her flesh smelling sweetly of the rose petals the maids had soaked into her bath. The fine, pale skin on her arms was marred with goosebumps although it was not cold. It was nervousness making the flesh stand up in tiny pimples, making her stomach quiver. This was her wedding night and she sat alone awaiting the bridegroom with whom she had exchanged not a word outside the marriage ceremony through which they had stood that afternoon.

They had danced to the minstrels' music after the wedding feast but that was all the contact they had shared. Sir Geoffrey's countenance was stern and he had not given her a smile of welcome; the one person who was smiling and congratulating himself was her father. He was delighted that one of his daughters was now entitled to be called 'My Lady'.

It seemed like hours since the maids left. Obviously her new husband was in no hurry to make her his wife; perhaps he was having too much fun with his friends in the great hall. She could still hear the music and laughter coming from the ground floor and she wondered how long it would continue before he grew bored and came to her bedchamber.

She was Lady Winterton now, just as her father wanted. He had searched for many months for an impoverished nobleman who would make her a lady in exchange for a generous dowry. Julia had no say in the chosen one, what manner of man he would be or whether she would even like him. That was the way of things and Sir Geoffrey Winterton had been the highest title to which her father could aspire. Just a man who had been knighted by the late King Henry for his service in battle, along with many others. Still it made her a lady and gave her access to the court, if her husband so desired.

Julia herself thought nothing of titles, or even much of wealth. She had never been without wealth, so she could hardly speak on that score, but the title was of no importance whatsoever. She was not like her younger sister in that respect; Bethany wanted a title and wealth, but she also wanted a man she could look up to and respect, just as Julia did. That was not too much to ask, was it? She hoped she could find those qualities in her husband.

She sighed heavily. Where was he? Why did he keep her waiting so long? It was insulting. She lie down and thought about the events of the day. First there had been the wedding service, a beautiful service written by Archbishop Thomas Cranmer himself. She had taken vows, so had Sir Geoffrey, and those vows had been dear to her. Her sister had come and wished her well, but Julia sensed she had her misgivings. Julia also had those misgivings, but she hoped she was wrong. Like most young maidens, she had read the romances and dreamed of a husband who would love her.

Eventually she fell asleep, still waiting for her bridegroom to join her, to complete the marriage. She awoke some hours later to feel hands, wet with sweat, touching her thighs, pushing up her shift, and she gasped in shock. In her deep slumber, she forgot for a moment that she was not at home in her own maidenly bedchamber, but was married now. Her eyes opened to nothing but darkness and the smell of wine on a man's breath.

She could see nothing, but she felt his hands pushing her legs apart, felt him roughly enter her body, felt the sharp pain and the movements of him, then the rapid end to his passion. She felt violated.

This was not what she had expected at all. She could not say what she had expected, as her mother told her nothing except that it would hurt and she told no lie. When he moved away from her, she watched as he swung his legs to the floor and stood up. He left the chamber without saying a word and her eyes filled with tears. Was this how it would be every night? She wondered. If he were going to be tender at all, this would surely be the night to be so; obviously this was indeed how it would be and she had no choice other than to endure such treatment.

She caught back a sob and buried her head in the pillow to weep away the humiliation and disappointment.

She had heard of some men having a 'reputation with the ladies' and wondered now what that reputation could be. Surely no woman would willingly give herself up to this unless she absolutely had to.

***

Julia's wedding night was likely the worst night of her life, but it seemed she was not to suffer such humiliation again. After a week of waiting for her husband to come once more to her bed, she gave up and thanked God for the respite.

She saw him at breakfast every morning, but he said nothing to her except a murmured greeting and a quick bow of his head. Eventually she began to get angry about that. She may not have a title of her own, she may be but a merchant's daughter, but she was well educated and had been treated with as much respect as a woman could expect before this. She saw no reason why that should end just because she had married this cold man.

She sat at the table, having finished her breakfast and waited for him to finish his before she spoke.

"Sir Geoffrey," she said. "I am unfamiliar with the customs of married people, but I thought you might have had a little more interest in your wife."

He was not a particularly attractive man but not hideous either. His skin was clear of blemishes, his hair an indiscriminate brownish colour, his beard the same. He was tall and very thin, which did not seem to be caused by lack of nourishment judging by the amount he ate, and since he had acquired his wife's fortune his clothing was rich and proved he had good taste in that regard.

Now he raised an eyebrow and his mouth turned down in distaste.

"I am sorry, My Lady," he answered with a heavy sigh. "I think perhaps we had better understand each other a little better and I have not been kind in keeping my thoughts to myself. I married you for your fortune; you know that so please do not look aghast and hurt."

His words angered her further, made her feel the need to retaliate.

"Yes, I know that," she said. "And I was made to marry you for your title, nothing more."

"Good. Then we have each gained what we wanted."

"What my father wanted."

"Ah, yes. You are a mere female and have no opinion." He sighed heavily. "The fact is, my dear, I have no interest in you or any woman. It was not only your fortune for which I married you, but for appearances also; people were beginning to talk. Now I have a wife, they will hopefully find someone else to gossip about."

Julia had no idea what he was talking about. Why should people talk? Why should they gossip about him, just because he lived alone and was unmarried? Many men lived in similar circumstances; but perhaps it was different for titled people.

Still, she did not understand why he said he had no interest in her.

"But you came to my bed," she said.

Again his mouth turned down in distaste.

"I did, although it was not the easiest thing I have ever had to do."

"Do you think that was enough to get you a son?" She demanded, hoping his answer would be in the affirmative. She did not want to experience that again. "I have been told a virgin cannot conceive the first time."

"That is of no importance to me," he answered harshly. "My brother is my heir and he satisfies me on that score."

"Then why did you make me suffer your disgusting attempt in the marriage bed?"

She could feel her voice rising but could do nothing about it and she saw his face flush with anger.

"Why?" He replied. "Because I did not want you running to the village priest with tales of non-consummation and divorcing me. I did not want you taking back your dowry."

Julia had nothing to say to that. She had no idea she could divorce him for that; she had no idea she could divorce him at all.

"You should have saved yourself the effort, Sir," she said bitterly. "My father would have been far more concerned with losing your title than in having to retrieve my dowry. That would be far more important to him than his daughter's happiness."

He looked at her and raised an eyebrow.

"You are likely right. He is an obsequious little man, a sycophant of the highest order."

Julia felt no offence at the slight to her father. In fact she rather agreed with him, but as he said, she was a mere female and had no opinion.

"So that is it?" She finally spoke. "That is our marriage, two separate people living separate lives under the same roof?"

He nodded.

"My Lady, you should be grateful. Your experience should have told you I can never make you happy and you can never give me what I need. I disgust you, I know it. I am used to that. I will give you enough respect, I will keep my friends away from your presence. All you need do is play the loving wife in public and you can live in this house, which is rather lovely I think, and call yourself Lady Winterton." He got to his feet before he added: "I think that is a fair exchange."

"Did my mother lie then? When she told me I was beautiful, did she lie?"

He watched her thoughtfully for a moment then gave her a half smile.

"You are very beautiful and I am sure very desirable," he answered. "But not to me. I regret that, do not think otherwise, but I can do nothing about it."

"I do not understand."

He pursed his lips thoughtfully then gave her a wistful smile.

"No, you really do not, do you? Perhaps you would be better remaining in ignorance. Suffice it to say, I will leave you in peace. You can close your pretty eyes and dream of whatever handsome man you want, as long as your dreams take no substance in reality. You can buy beautiful clothes, wear beautiful jewels and ride a beautiful horse. But you will be my wife in name only. I am sorry; that is the way it is."

"But I am not to take a lover?" She demanded as he turned to go. "If you do not want me, why should you care?"

He turned back and stood beside the table, close to her so she had to bend her head back to see his face.

"I married you to still gossiping tongues. Your loyalty is required to maintain that image and I will have that loyalty, make no mistake."

He turned back to the door and strode away, while she watched him go and swallowed back yet another tear. As she thought about it, she wondered if she would be better off. She would never know love, but she would have her life to herself. It was the best of a bad bargain, but how could she live with a man who had no interest in her? And why did he have no interest in her? He was right – she did not understand and was not sure she ever wanted to.

CHAPTER TWO

Winterton House was, as its owner had said, beautiful. It was by no means the largest house she had lived in, certainly not as large as her father's country manor or even his London residence, but it was a reasonable size and since there would be only the two of them, it would suit. There would be no need to add extra rooms for a nursery, extra apartments for nurses and nursery maids. No need for a ballroom to provide a court when the children grew up and marriages needed to be arranged.

Perhaps that was for the best. Julia wondered how she would feel about that, if she should ever have a daughter, considering her present unhappy state. Still, she had always wanted to have children. She believed she would make a good mother.

She gathered her cloak about her as she looked up at the house. Autumn was coming; she wondered what sort of Christmas Sir Geoffrey would keep at his manor house; would that be one of the occasions she was to play the loving wife? How would that play out? With guests staying they might expect Sir Geoffrey and Lady Winterton to share a bedchamber. The notion brought with it a shudder of distaste.

The chill in the air made Julia want to make the most of these last summer days and explore the grounds and surrounding areas. She had little else to do.

The house stood alone in the centre of formal gardens with flowers and shrubs, yew hedges and cut grass. It would be lovely in the summer, a lovely place to sit and read or merely to think.

She was curious about the huge mansion whose grounds touched the edge of Winterton land. She asked Sir Geoffrey about it and was rewarded with a scowl of displeasure.

"Your best option is to stay well clear of its owner," he replied.

What was this, a spark of jealousy?

"Why?"

"He has a bad reputation," he replied.

Ah, one of those men who had a reputation, but for what she still found puzzling.

"For what?"

He stared at her thoughtfully for a little while, then the scowl turned to a flash of anger.

"I am telling you to stay away from him," he said. "That is all you need to know."

Obviously there was much more she wanted to know, even if the need was absent. She went to the stables and chose a small pony to take her on her short journey. She was not much of a rider, but being out here she needed the practice.

As she approached the edge of Winterton land, she saw in the distance a rider on a tall, black horse coming toward her. She drew rein and stopped to watch him; he looked as though he was aiming straight for her, but she could hardly think that to be the case. Yet he kept coming and she wondered if this was the owner of the mansion, she wondered what he would say if she were to encroach on his land.

She was still wondering when he drew rein beside her.

"Richard Summerville," he said with a small bow of his head. "You must be the new Lady Winterton."

She had been expecting someone much older and Geoffrey's warning about his reputation suddenly made sense. She could guess what that reputation was for. He was very handsome, very well built and with a lovely smile which shone like the sunlight on his dark hair.

She admitted that he made her heart skip a beat; he could have stepped straight out of those romances she was so fond of, a Sir Lancelot to her Guinevere, perhaps? She loved those stories.

"I suppose I must be," she replied.

"I am delighted to meet you. I was hoping for a glimpse when I rode this way."

"You were?" He nodded. "Why?"

He gave her that lovely smile again.

"I had heard my neighbour had won himself a beautiful bride and I was curious to see if that rumour was true."

She ducked her head and smiled a little shyly.

"And was it?" She murmured.

"Indeed it was, and you, My Lady, are fishing for compliments."

She laughed then, for the first time since her father had told her of the match he had made for her. If this man had a reputation with the ladies, she could well understand it. She no longer wondered why her husband ordered her to stay away from him. If people were inclined to gossip, this man would definitely be at the centre of such gossip.

"I am glad I made you laugh," Richard said. "You looked a little lost when I rode up."

"I am a little lost, My Lord. This is all very strange to me, living out here, being married."

"Ah, yes. Your marriage." He paused and gazed at her for a few moments before he asked, as though he already knew the answer: "Do you think you will be happy together?"

She flushed, turned her head away.

"It is early days."

He reached across the space between them and touched her hand gently. The gesture held such tenderness, she almost cried.

***

Sir Geoffrey might have acquired his fortune through marriage, but he was not ungenerous with it. Julia suspected his generosity to be more for the benefit of others, to give the impression of a loving husband, than any genuine benevolence.

She had ordered a virginals to play, she had many fine clothes and he had even gone with her to buy her own pony. That was a gesture she had not expected, even if he did have to bring his friend with him.

Maxwell was his name, and he looked more like a girl in man's clothing than a grown man. Geoffrey kept smiling at him and he returned the look with adoration in his green eyes. Julia shuddered; what a horrible sight that was. He was almost leering and were Geoffrey a woman instead of a man, she would have thought there was a secret there.

"Why did we have to bring your friend?" She asked.

"Because he knows a lot about horses, my dear," he replied. "I do not want to make a mistake and have you endanger yourself on a horse which is too strong or unschooled."

"Would that not be to your advantage? You have my fortune; what need have you now for a wife?"

He smiled, a cruel smile, a smile she imagined the Roman emperors displayed when watching Christians being thrown to the lions, or watching gladiators fight to the death.

"I have need of a wife to secure my position and still gossiping tongues. I already told you. If harm were to befall you, I would have to begin again with a new wife. You know how disagreeable that would be." He turned back to the paddock to watch the herd. "Have you made up your mind which one you like?"

There was a little palomino mare who seemed to be calling to her. She was not grazing like the others; she was standing still near the fence and her eyes followed Julia wherever she went.

"That one," she pointed.

Geoffrey turned to his friend in enquiry.

"She looks like a good choice," Maxwell said.

He opened the paddock gate and went inside, called to the mare with his hand held out and she immediately trotted towards him and rubbed her nose into his palm. Julia smiled. She may not like this friend of her husband's, but quite obviously the equine population thought highly of him.

He led her out of the paddock and handed the rein to Julia, who led her away to find a saddle and bridle while the two men smiled fondly at each other.

Recalling her earlier thoughts of Camelot, Julia named the little mare Guinevere, after King Arthur's Queen, and she was delighted with her. She spent the afternoon playing with her, grooming her, riding about the estate and the Summerville lands. The Earl had been kind enough to invite her to ride his lands whenever she wanted and when she was not doing that, she spent her time playing her instrument and sewing. At least there was no one to tell her how to behave all the time, as before her marriage, but in truth she missed having someone who was that interested in her.

Her father had ideas of how the nobility behaved and he tried to instil those ideas into his daughters, but from what Julia had discovered so far, he was wrong in his assumptions.

She saw little of Geoffrey, but the night the first frost covered the grass, he was waiting for her at the supper table.

A fire had been lit and the logs burned brightly, the flames leaping up into the chimney and making the whole atmosphere friendly. Darkness was falling, candles had been lit and Geoffrey waved a letter at her as she sat down.

"Your father requests we accommodate your sister for the festive period," he told her. "He hopes she might meet a man of consequence among our Christmas guests."

He gave a derogatory laugh.

"And your answer will be?"

"What else can it be but 'yes'? Although I think he will be disappointed. I cannot see much hope for his plan among my friends."

"For Bethany's sake, I hope you are right," Julia answered bitterly. "I wish for more for my sister than my own fate."

Geoffrey looked at her sharply, a flush of anger on his face.

"You could do a lot worse, my dear," he said at last. "You could have fallen in love, given your heart to an unfaithful lover. That is surely more painful than the indifference of someone you hardly know."

"Is that what happened to you? Is that why you are so cold?"

He smiled cynically, as though her question had amused him.

"Alas, I have never had the privilege." He paused and his eyes bored into her until she looked away to hide her discomfort. "You really do not know, do you?" He went on.

"Know what?"

He shrugged.

"No matter," he said. "I saw you riding toward Summerville Hall yesterday. Please do not go there again."

"Why not? His Lordship was kind enough to give me permission to ride on his lands."

"You have spoken to him?" Geoffrey snapped, his voice rising. "I told you to stay away from him. I will not tell you again."

Her heart jumped fearfully, but she saw no reason to blindly obey. If a man wanted obedience from his wife, he should offer something in return. Respect and deference must be earned, even from a mere woman.

"What have you against him, Sir?" She persisted. "I saw him this morning, with his wife. She is very beautiful, not a woman I could distract him from, I am certain."

He reached out and took her hand, making her think his heart had softened, but he squeezed her hand so tightly he crushed her bones and made her cry out and fight to snatch it away from his grip. Still he held tight.

"Please," she cried out. "You will break my hand."

He released her, threw her hand away from him as though it were something hateful.

"She is not his wife," he said at last. "She is his mistress. His favourite of many from what I have heard and you are right; you would never compete with the lovely Rachel. It is best not to try."

She rubbed her injured hand to soothe it, her mouth turned down to suppress the threatened tears.

"Why do you hate him so much?"

"That is my concern, not yours. Just do as you are told and do not go there again. I do not want to have to curb your freedom, but I will if it becomes necessary."

He pushed back his bench so that it scraped across the floor and got to his feet, but before he left the hall he reached out and pinched her cheeks between his rough fingers, pinched them hard, squeezing her mouth out of shape. She would not plead with him a second time; once was all her pride could tolerate for one evening.

***

The following day Julia watched from her window as her husband rode away from the house. She had no idea where he was going, where he went most days, and she no longer cared. Quite obviously he had no interest in her, not even to provide him with a son, but given that she could not understand his apparent jealousy of his neighbour. Perhaps it was his wealth which angered him, or that he was far more handsome and attractive to women. Perhaps it was his superior title, his vast lands so close to Winterton lands, which Geoffrey could only gaze upon with avarice.

Whatever it was, it was certain his hatred was real and not fuelled by jealousy of Julia. Her husband had no interest in his wife as a woman, that was apparent and she still had no idea why. She had always been told she was beautiful, that any man would be mad with desire for her. Her best assumption was that he had a mistress somewhere, someone he could not marry but whose company he preferred to that of his wife.

But what manner of woman would want to endure his fumbling attentions?

He would be gone all day, he always was, and she wondered if perhaps he had ordered one of the servants to watch her movements or maybe he assumed she would simply follow his orders. But she had no intention of doing so.

She dressed in a new winter gown of red velvet and covered herself with a white fur cloak, as protection against the cold. Outside she tacked up Guinevere herself and rode her toward the forbidden lands next door. She was intrigued and determined to learn the cause of Sir Geoffrey's hatred.

She had never been inside the house, but today she rode right up to the solid oak front doors. A stable hand came running to help her dismount and take her mare away to the stables and as soon as her feet touched the ground, the door opened and a manservant stood waiting to lead her inside.

It was as though she were expected, but she could not believe that was true. This must be how His Lordship's servants were trained to greet visitors and she could not help but be impressed.

She was offered a seat inside the door, a polished oak settle with embroidered cushions for comfort. As she waited, she felt a little guilty about disobeying her husband. She had been raised to believe she should always be loyal to him and follow his wishes, no matter what, and she had deliberately come here against those express wishes. It was not even as though she could pretend she misunderstood, but had he been in the least bit interested in her she might have respected her duty to the man she had married. As it was, she felt no particular loyalty to him. Since the day they wed the only feeling he had aroused in her was self pity, misery and disgust.

At last she heard a footstep on the stair and turned to face her illustrious neighbour, who rewarded her with that appealing smile. Her heart hammered; what was she doing? Why was she here and what on earth could she say to him?

"Delighted," he said at once, stepping forward and taking her hand.

As he raised it to his lips and kissed it, his eyes met hers and he turned to his servant and ordered refreshments, then he led her into his sitting room and closed the door.

"Forgive me, My Lord," she said hesitantly. "I am not really sure why I came here."

"Richard, please. I hate titles."

"Richard."

"You need no reason to visit me, My Lady," he said. "I am always happy to see a beautiful woman."

She swallowed hard to give herself courage. She should not be here, her husband had forbidden it, and she should not be so forthright as to ask the Earl his reason. At least that is what her father had told her, but she had to know and there seemed but one way to find out.

She suddenly thought of her sister and a smile forced itself to her lips. If Bethany wanted to know something, if she were in her place now, she would simply ask. Father had always scolded her about her outspoken ways, her forthrightness. But Julia did not find it so easy to be outspoken and she hesitated, concerned about his reaction.

The servant returned with wine, bread and cheese, and as soon as he had left she spoke immediately.

"My husband forbade me to come here," she said quickly, before her courage failed her. "I would like to know why."

Bethany would be proud, but she felt her cheeks begin to flame. He moved subtly away from her and studied her face.

"Perhaps he is jealous," he suggested.

"Would that were the case," she answered, her cheeks burning even hotter. "He has shown no interest in me whatsoever, so why should he care? I do not know, but I believe you do."

He put his arm around her shoulders and held her close to him, while her heart hammered painfully. She had never known this sort of closeness with a man before, especially one so attractive, and the disappointment of the past few weeks had made her vulnerable to those qualities.

His hand touched her face, held her cheek gently. He was going to kiss her; she knew he was going to kiss her and she knew she should move away, object to his closeness, but she did not want to. It would be nice to know how the kiss of a man might taste.

His lips met hers and she felt she was going to fall. She could do nothing but respond to his kiss with one of her own.

"So much beauty wasted on such a creature," he murmured. "That is the tragedy."

"What do you mean?" He made no reply and she swallowed her nervousness, pulled away from him to meet his gaze with her own. "I do not know you, My Lord, but I feel you will be honest with me. I was forced to marry a man I knew nothing about and I thought we would grow close, at least try to develop a relationship. But it has not happened and I want to know why. What do I have to do to make myself more desirable to him?"

He pulled her toward him again, held her in his arms and kissed her cheek. Then he sighed.

"Nothing," he answered. "There is nothing you can do. He is a deviant, a sodomite."

She pushed herself away and stared up into his face.

"What does that mean?"

"It means, my dear, he is a mistake, an error of nature, a man who is attracted to his own sex."

She gasped and her hand fled to cover her mouth, her eyes opened so wide she thought they might pop out of her head. She could not remember when she had ever been so shocked.

She pulled herself farther away from him, slid along the polished wood of the settle to leave a space between them. She could not think if she were that close to him and she needed to think, desperately. He had to be lying, he simply had to be.

"You lie!" She cried. "There is no such thing. Why are you trying to frighten me?"

"I am sorry to have to be the one to enlighten you, but I speak the truth. I can even find the passage in the Bible which forbids such relationships; why would the holy book even mention it, if no such thing existed?"

Her vision was blurred now, her eyes swimming in the tears she had held on to these past weeks. She had hoped, despite Geoffrey's indifference, to tempt him. Even despite his fumbling on their wedding night, she hoped to make things better and now she was being assured he was some sort of monster.

Richard took her hand, brought it to his lips and pulled her close to him again.

"I am sorry," he said.

"That is why he never comes to my bed?"

"You can divorce him for that, you know. But it would be very public."

She could only stare at him. She believed him, but had no idea why she believed him. He had no reason to tell her such a lie, he had no reason to invent such a tale.

"I am sorry," he said gently. "You really had no idea, did you?"

She shook her head and frantically tried to wipe away the tears with her fingers.

"So it is hopeless then," she muttered. "I have no marriage. My father would likely never believe me and even if he did, he would never allow a divorce. Geoffrey would not return my dowry and I would be penniless and cast out. I am trapped."

He held her close to comfort her and she felt an unaccustomed need to kiss him. She reached her lips to meet his and he kissed her again and she had no thought of resisting; she did not want to resist him. This was what she wanted, even if it proved to be only fleeting.

When he released her he kept his arm around her shoulders, leaned back in his seat and allowed her head to rest on his chest.

This woman was very beautiful, very desirable, but he did not want to take advantage of her unhappiness. And he needed to be sure his desire was for her, not for some twisted vengeance on her husband whom he had always loathed. He made a tremendous effort to offer nothing other than comfort.

Julia closed her eyes and smelled the masculinity coming from this man. His arm around her was making her feel so good, his kiss had produced an unfamiliar throbbing in her groin and this new knowledge about her husband was making her want to do something to spite him.

Were these good enough reasons for her next words?

"You have a mistress," she said against his chest. "At least that is what Geoffrey told me."

"I do. Why do you ask?"

"Is she exclusive? Would she be heartbroken if you were unfaithful to her?"

He laughed then, but she felt no threat. He was not laughing at her, which is what she feared, but at the notion of Rachel expecting fidelity from him.

"No," he said. "Rachel does not love me and I do not love her. We suit each other, nothing more."

"She does not live here?"

He shook his head.

"She did for a time, until her own house was built." He felt her heart thumping against his chest. "What are you asking me?"

She blushed, her cheeks burning and glowing crimson and she could say nothing for a few moments.

"I want you to show me what it is supposed to be like," she finally said. "Geoffrey says you have a reputation; he did not say for what, but I have a good idea."

He smiled and kissed her, then pulled her to her feet and led her from the room and up the wide staircase.

Inside his bedchamber he locked the door and turned to her, held her chin in his fingers and gently guided her face up to look at him.

"Are you sure this is what you want?" He asked. "I do not want to take advantage of you, of your vulnerability and your need of affection."

"I am sure," she replied, nodding.

"If we do this, it will lead nowhere; you realise that? I will not change my allegiance and be faithful to you, I will not take you away from your husband and I will not give my heart to you."

She grinned a little.

"You are very arrogant, Sir, to think I might want all those things."

He laughed, then unlaced her bodice, removed her clothes and let them fall to the floor. He unfastened his breeches and stood in only his silk shirt, held her close against him and kissed her again as he pushed her onto his bed.

A sudden stab of guilt shot through her. She recalled Geoffrey's angry face when he ordered her to stay away from this man and she knew she had come here as a gesture of defiance. But it was too late to turn back now, was it not?

She remembered those vows she had made in the small village church, vows of fidelity, vows to remain constant to him.

"This is wrong," she murmured.

"A woman as lovely as you was made to be loved, not to be an ornament, a token bride for an unnatural man. But the choice is yours. You can stop me any time you wish, but please do not leave it too long."

As he held her head close to his naked chest, she had a sudden urge to kiss that chest and some demon inside her decided not to fight that urge. He held her close, kissed her neck, her shoulders, trailed his lips down to take her breast into his mouth as his fingers stroked her body.

She found herself longing for each touch, for each kiss; she returned each caress with one of her own and her eyes filled with tears of joy when she felt him inside her, as he clung to her and pulled her so close she thought she might meld with him.

After, he kissed her again before moving away and gathering her into his arms.

"Thank you," she said softly. "Thank you so much."

"It is I who should thank you. What a pity I did not see you before Winterton claimed you."

She laughed, for the first time in weeks.

"You are teasing me, My Lord," she said. "But that is all right. You have given me something today, something I would never have known without you. You have made me feel like a real woman again, and I will be forever grateful."

***

Julia smiled to herself on her way back to Winterton House, images of the afternoon racing through her memory, the afternoon she had spent in her neighbour's bed. During the weeks leading up to her marriage, she had been excited and apprehensive at the same time, but she had promised herself she would be a good wife. It seems she had broken that promise already and she felt a little guilty about that, but when she compared her wedding night with this afternoon she thought she could be pardoned. It would not happen again; His Lordship was very tempting, but she could not risk conceiving a child as Geoffrey would know it was not his and she shuddered to think what he would do. Why had she not thought of that before now? It had never crossed her mind, never found a place amid the longing for something which had been denied her.

One day, if it please the Lord, she would be free of Geoffrey and find someone who knew how to treat a woman. She cared nothing for a title or a doorway into society; those were her father's dreams, not hers. All she wanted was a man who would love her; was that really too much to ask?

When she arrived home, Sir Geoffrey was waiting for her. He never waited for her, never cared enough to wait for her, but this evening he waited in the hall and she knew at once she had been discovered.

"Where have you been?" He demanded.

"Just for a ride."

"A ride to Summerville Hall," he answered. "I saw you."

His jaw was clenched, as were his fists, and she felt suddenly terrified. She turned and began to flee to the door, but he caught up with her in one stride and grabbed her upper arm, pinching viciously into her flesh. He spun her around and slapped her face, hard.

"I told you to keep away from that man!"

Tears clouded her vision, but the need to fight back was overpowering.

"Why?" She said, holding her injured face. "You do not want me, so why should I not seek affection elsewhere?"

"You are my wife. You will obey me. I will not have you sneaking off to that Papist adulterer and making me look a fool."

She stared at him, her eyes scrutinising his face in the hope of seeing deception, but all she saw was rage.

"Papist?" She repeated.

"Ah, he did not tell you." He dropped her arm and turned away, went back to the table to finish his meal. "You will remain in the house from now on," he said. "Until our Christmas festivities at any rate. Do not think to leave; you will look more than a little foolish if the servants have to restrain you."

"You would lock me in, like a common prisoner?"

"I would."

She approached the table and stood looking down at him.

"If Lord Summerville is a Catholic and you quite obviously detest him, why do you not report him?"

His eyes narrowed as they met hers.

"You will keep quiet about it," he said. "If it gets out, there are things about me he knows which I would prefer to keep private."

"You mean your peculiar tastes, I suppose," Julia spat at him.

He leapt to his feet, grabbed her arm and twisted it painfully.

"I knew he would tell you," he said. "You will keep quiet about that too, or you may learn whether purgatory exists sooner than you expected."

***

Bethany arrived in their father's carriage, beautifully dressed in the most expensive fabric a merchant's daughter was allowed. It was an odd thing that he had made a fortune dealing in the cloth which his class was forbidden to wear. Her dark hair shone in the afternoon sunlight; Julia had often wondered why her sister's hair was so dark, whilst her own was very fair, almost white. Perhaps it was a throwback from her ancient origins, but it was merely a passing thought.

Julia ran out to meet her as the carriage drew to a halt. She was truly delighted to see her, to have someone who cared for her welfare and her happiness in the house and to have someone to talk to. She had been shut up in this house since her visit to her neighbour, but Geoffrey would not do that with her sister here. What would the gossips say?

"Welcome," she said, taking her hands as she stepped down. "Did you have a good journey?"

Bethany gave her a dazzling smile, her dark eyes sparkling with excitement.

"It was comfortable," she replied. "But far too long. Why did you have to move so far away from me?"

"You talk as though I had an opinion in the matter."

Bethany pulled her close and hugged her.

"Forgive me," she said. "I was not thinking. I wish you had fought harder though. I intend to."

"What good will that do? You have to marry someone; Father will accept no man who will not aid him up the social ladder."

"We shall see. You are looking very pale, Julia, even more than usual. Are you quite well?"

Julia nodded. She knew why she was looking pale, she knew why she was sick most mornings and she knew that as soon as this visit was over, she would have to confess to her lover that she was carrying his child. She could not pass it off as Geoffrey's, could she?

Since their afternoon together, Julia had discovered that His Lordship had more mistresses than Rachel. Perhaps he could be persuaded to add her to them, find her somewhere safe to live with her child. Or perhaps he would support her for no return, considering the child was his. She did not know him well enough to know how he would react. She had been interested in his skills in the bedchamber, not his character.

Bethany was chattering away and Julia forced her attention back to her. The visit would be over in but a few weeks, then she could make plans.

"Do you have many guests coming, my dear?" She was saying. "Are there lots of titled gentlemen for father to feel pleased about?"

"A few," Julia replied, but her thoughts were on the list of guests her husband had given her with instructions of who to invite and when.

"The Earl of Summerville?" She had seen his name at the bottom of the list, to be invited for twelfth night.

"Yes," Geoffrey replied. "Unfortunately, he owns half the county; it would be socially unacceptable not to invite him. I invite him every year, but he never comes. It is merely a formality, so you need have no fear his presence will embarrass you."

She had been relieved to know he was unlikely to show himself, but so far there had been no reply from him.

"Well?" Bethany prompted her. "Are there many impoverished noblemen for me to choose from?"

"Some," came the voice of Sir Geoffrey, who had stepped up behind his wife and now gently rested his hand on her shoulder. So the façade had begun already, Julia thought. Bethany curtsied.

"Sir Geoffrey."

Once inside the house, refreshments were ordered for their guest and Geoffrey excused himself.

"I expect you have much to talk to your sister about," he commented as he kissed Julia's cheek. She flinched; she could not help it and she was sure Bethany noticed.

Bethany reached across the table and took her sister's hand.

"You do not seem happy, my dear," she said soothingly.

"Happiness was not something I expected."

"But you should," Bethany replied heatedly. "You are entitled to be happy. Why should we be pawns in Father's game?"

"It was that or be turned out to starve," Julia replied. "The deed is done now. I can only hope for better things for my little sister."

CHAPTER THREE

Julia's heart bounced in her chest when she saw him enter the great hall. Her glance moved to Geoffrey where he sat at the table with some guests and she saw his angry scowl when the steward announced 'His Lordship, The Earl of Summerville'.

"What is he doing here?" She muttered.

"Was he not invited?" Bethany asked excitedly.

"Oh yes," she answered as she walked hurriedly toward the new guest. "He is our nearest and most important neighbour. He has to be invited, but he never comes; never."

She did not hear her sister's reply but a quick glance told her Geoffrey was watching her, studying her every move.

She had not been able to leave the house without Bethany and before her arrival, had been confined like a prisoner. It was degrading to be so treated before the servants, but she supposed she deserved it.

No opportunity had presented itself for her to visit her neighbour and tell him of her condition, beg him for his help. Now she found herself close to him, she could not speak for fear of being overheard.

"My Lord," she whispered urgently. "Why are you here?"

"You invited me."

"I have to speak to you. It is very important."

His eyes moved past her as though his attention had been drawn away and she turned to see her sister standing behind her. Damn! Just as she had got his attention. She could do nothing but present Bethany to him and hope for another opportunity to speak with him in private.

The remainder of that evening was for Julia nerve racking as she watched the Earl employ his considerable charm on her sister. She wondered what they could possibly have to talk about, coming from such totally different worlds as they did, and her own encounter with him consisted of little conversation. She felt suddenly ashamed of that; she knew nothing about this man, nothing at all. According to Geoffrey, he was a Papist and she was a married woman. Yet she had spent an afternoon in his bed and enjoyed every minute.

Recalling that afternoon, she felt a sudden flash of concern about Bethany. She had to find a moment to warn her, before she fell under his spell. He seemed like a caring man, one who would do nothing dishonourable, yet he had bedded his neighbour's wife without hesitation. But she had asked him to, had she not? Could he be trusted with a virgin? Would he hesitate to take that jewel from her then leave her to return to her life as it was? Julia had no idea. She would have refused to consider it had Geoffrey not told her of his religious leanings. As far as Julia was concerned, there could be no greater evil. Papists had no morals, no principles and she felt more ashamed of what she had done with one of them than she had ever felt when he was merely her wealthy neighbour.

***

Little progress was made with the business of finding a husband for Bethany. Geoffrey seemed to think it highly amusing, whilst Julia just wanted to put her into the carriage and send her back to London so she could sneak out and talk to Lord Summerville. He would help her. Surely being a Papist would not prevent that, would it? Since she had learned of that she was not nearly so confident of his support, but it would be his child; surely he would want to support his own child, especially as he had no others. At least as far as she knew he had no others, but her own predicament assured her it was a possibility not to be ignored.

Her mind was full of ideas about how he would react, what his solution would be. Would he find her somewhere to live, away from here? She was sure he must have other houses, being as he was obviously wealthy. Titled people of wealth always had many estates and houses all over the country. He had said he would not take her away from her husband, she remembered that, but surely if she were in danger he would change his mind. If his child were in danger he would want to help, surely.

Would he be angry? He had no right to be angry, did he? Oh, why did time not hurry? She could bear this uncertainly no more.

She had been sick again that morning and this time Geoffrey had noticed. How galling that she could dress as provocatively as she could, brush her pale hair until it was as soft as silk and shone in the sunlight, yet he never noticed at all. But he had proved himself no fool; he may have no interest in women, but he was apparently aware of how their bodies functioned.

He was waiting for her when she came back inside the house.

"What ails you, My Lady?" He asked.

Could he be persuaded the child was his? She wondered. He did come to her bed on their wedding night and perhaps the tale was wrong that a virgin could not conceive the first time. Or perhaps, if he believed the tale, he would accuse her of not being a maid. She knew he could be vicious and she had to ask herself how far that trait would go. But it was three months into her marriage before this child was conceived; there was no hope of persuading her husband it was his progeny.

"Well?" He persisted.

"I have eaten of too much rich food, Sir," she replied at last. "Nothing more. I will be better when we return to normal meals."

She watched him go out then turned to where Bethany was just descending the staircase. She would be on her way home today, leaving Julia free to see Richard and seek his support. Her sister's greeting as she reached the bottom of the stairs crumbled her plans to dust, made her feel she was drowning and could not quite reach the surface and safety.

"What do you mean, he has offered you marriage?" She demanded.

"Just as I say. Lord Summerville has made me an offer of marriage and I am going to Summerville Hall now to accept him."

Panic clutched at Julia's heart and squeezed painfully and she felt her eyes widen, felt the colour drain from her face. What would she do if Bethany married the father of her child? He was her only hope, her one salvation. She could not marry him! She simply could not!

"You cannot marry him!"

"Why not?"

Julia could not answer that. All her hopes of gaining his help, of seeking his support drained away from her. She had to persuade her sister to refuse him; it would be too dishonourable to take her sister's husband as her protector, possibly as her lover.

"He will never be faithful to you."

"I know that. I care nothing for him, so what is that to me?" Bethany held her hands, tried to pull her toward her but she stood fast. "How can I refuse him? He offers so much."

"He is a Papist!" Julia spat. "Did he tell you that?"

"He did."

Something in Julia's heart turned to stone. She hated the Catholic Church, she wanted them all dead for the torture and barbarism they had inflicted in the past. They held the souls of men and women hostage with their superstitious nonsense, with their arrogant assumption that they could control the afterlife, that they could charge money for a swift passage through a fictitious place they called purgatory.

She felt sullied enough for having allowed one of them to bed her, to be having his child was something she would keep from him if she had a choice, but to accept him as the husband of her dear sister was just too much.

"Please, Bethany, do not do this. He will not allow you to keep your own beliefs; he will expect you to follow his superstitions, his Catholic dogma. Does his wealth and title mean that much to you?"

Bethany turned her face away, but not before Julia had seen the crimson flush which crossed her cheeks.

"You will turn for his wealth?" Julia demanded.

"Why do you care?" Bethany asked. "It is not you who is being asked to change her beliefs."

"Because you will burn in hell and I will never see you again." She could say no more; the words would not form, could not get passed the ache in her throat. At last the ache cleared enough for just one condemnation. "Go! Make your dirty bargain with the Earl. You are no sister to me."

***

The weeks leading up to the wedding were torture for Julia. She wanted desperately to run away, but Geoffrey watched her every move. He knew, she was sure of it. He had been a little too eager to attend the marriage of his hated neighbour and he watched her the whole time they were there.

"You had best talk to your sister," he told her. "Wish her well."

"What is it to you? You care nothing for her happiness, or his."

"I care that if you do not behave like a loving sister, someone is going to wonder why. Do you want her to know what a whore you are? Do you want her to know what manner of man she is about to wed?"

She had no answer for him; she only wondered if the knowledge would be enough to deter Bethany from her goal. She had accepted his mistresses, his religion; would she also accept this? Julia had a strong suspicion that she would, that she would not give up the Earl and his wealth, even if she was told her own sister was carrying his child.

Julia felt cold toward Bethany now; all this talk of marrying her to a stranger for a title had turned her from the sweet girl she once was into someone who would sell her soul for wealth and power.

And what had Geoffrey planned for the future? He would not allow her to keep the child, that was for certain. He would take it away, abandon it somewhere whilst she lie helpless from the birth. She could not allow that to happen; she had to get away somehow.

She thought of telling her father that the Earl he was so pleased about was a hated Catholic, but that would mean imprisonment for Richard and the loss of all his lands and wealth. She did not want him to suffer. He had given her something special and she would be forever thankful. Geoffrey would not betray his secret either, for fear of his own secrets being revealed.

***

Julia expected her sister to visit her at the first opportunity, but she was relieved when she made no appearance at Winterton House. She had been dreading the encounter; her figure was swelling and she was sure Bethany would notice. Of course, she would think the child Sir Geoffrey's, but Julia had nothing to say to her. She had still not forgiven her choice and she was not sure she ever could. She had asked herself many times if she would have done differently, given the same choice, and each time the answer was 'yes'. Julia was devout and would tolerate anything rather than become a Papist.

A few days after the wedding, Geoffrey came to her bedchamber as the maidservant left. It was the first time he had set foot inside since their wedding night and she was quite sure he had not made the effort to make a further attempt at his fumbling advances.

She had just climbed into bed and now she pulled the covers up over herself and watched as he closed the door and stood leaning against it for a moment, that cruel smile on his face once more.

"Why have you come?" She said. "Has the wedding given you romantic thoughts?"

He made no reply, just strode quickly to the bed and pulled the covers from her. His eyes moved over her and he reached out a hand and traced a line over the slight bulge of her stomach.

"You are with child," he said. "It is Summerville's bastard?"

She did not reply, just bit her lip to stop the tears which were gathering, threatening to overflow.

"What do you care?" She answered at last. "You can pretend you are a real man if I have a child."

His jaw clenched and his eyes narrowed as he raised his hand and slapped her face, hard enough to form a bruise by morning.

She let out a scream and he grabbed her face and squeezed it tight to silence her, then he pushed her away, her head bounced on the pillow behind her and he took her wrist and twisted it painfully.

"Had you told me earlier, I could have helped you," he said.

"You? How?"

"I could have found someone to get rid of it. As it is, I will have to allow it to grow, to fester like a parasite until it tears you apart to give itself life."

His mouth formed a grimace of distaste as he spoke, but still his words gave her hope.

"So you will allow the child to be born?"

"I have no choice," he replied. "But do not begin to plan a nursery. As soon as it breathes its first, it will be gone. I will not have that man's brat in my house."

She began to shake her head, the tears finally winning and flooding down her injured face.

"You will not take my child."

"I will smother the bastard; trust me on that. It will not breathe life for long."

The instinct for maternal protection fought with self pity and won.

"And what do you think Richard will do when he learns that you murdered his child?"

He towered above her, fury staining his flesh to crimson.

"Richard, is it now?" He said mockingly. "Well, you will not leave this house again to tell him, be sure of that. He will never know what happened to his brat and if you defy me again, he will never know what happened to its mother either."

She watched him go, jumped as the door slammed behind him. She had no choice now. She could not seek help from the child's father because he had married her sister; she could not stay here where her child would be murdered. No doubt Geoffrey would accept all the condolences of the neighbourhood and his friends, no doubt he would play the attentive husband and cherish each moment of the attention.

She cried herself to sleep that night, but in the morning she packed as many of her clothes as she could manage, took the jewels which Geoffrey had given her to give the impression of being a devoted husband and stuffed them into the travelling bag along with her gowns.

She heard a horse galloping away from the house and glanced out of the window to see him riding away towards Norwich and his latest paramour. If that was where he was going, he would be gone all day and now she began to feel some of the spite which seemed to come naturally to her husband.

She put her bag under the bed and went across the gallery to the bedchamber occupied by Sir Geoffrey. She had never been in here before and now she stopped and looked around at the pictures which covered the walls. There were a lot of them, paintings and sketches, all of handsome young men in erotic pose.

Julia shuddered and went to the cabinet beside the bed. It was not locked; doubtless he thought that unnecessary, that she would not dare to invade his privacy like this. He was wrong. She bent down and withdrew the leather chest from inside. This was locked, but she shook it a little to be sure the family jewels, the jewels which had been in the Winterton family for generations, were there. Why should she not have them? Had she not suffered for them?

Had he been content with threatening and mistreating her, she would never had thought to rob him; once he threatened her baby everything changed.

On a side table she found a knife, an ornate dagger with a jewelled handle. She held fast to the chest and plunged the tip of the dagger into the lock, pulled as hard as she could to tear the leather on the catch and opened it to see the beautiful jewels her husband had briefly shown her just after their wedding. She thought he was going to present them to her; what a fool!

She gathered them up and shoved them into a velvet purse she carried with her, then she picked up the dagger and pushed it into the purse as well. She would either use it as a weapon or she would sell it; it was obviously valuable.

Downstairs, she opened the window and dropped the travelling bag out onto the ground behind the shrubs which grew against the house. She wanted none of the servants to see her with it.

Outside, she ran to the stables and tacked up Guinevere herself, looked around to be sure she was not seen, then collected her travelling bag and rode away. As she passed Summerville Hall she slowed, wondering if there was still a way to tell Richard about her predicament, about the child. It was not as though Bethany loved him, was it? It was not as though she had not accepted him for what he was; it would surely come as no surprise to her.

She gathered what little courage she could muster and hoped she could find him alone. She had no time to waste, but she was making her way at a steady pace toward the house when she saw in the distance two people walking in the grounds. From here, she thought at first glance the woman was Richard's mistress, with her dark hair and perfect figure, and she was offended on her sister's behalf. He was married now; he should not have the woman in his house while his wife was there. That was disrespectful, no matter what their agreement.

But as she drew closer she realised it was Bethany and she saw that the couple were holding hands. As she watched they stopped walking and turned to each other; he drew her into his arms and kissed her while she clung to him as though she would meld with him, just as Julia felt she would meld with him when he had kissed her. But not here, in the open? This was very different to the foreplay to an afternoon of passion.

She could scarcely believe this was her independent and outspoken sister. What on earth had happened to her in the few days since her marriage to this man? Julia already knew he was charming and handsome, she also knew about his skills with women, knew first hand, but it seemed Bethany had fallen completely under his spell.

No, she could not tell him. Obviously the unforeseen had happened; her sister was in love with this man. Julia was still angry with her for marrying a Papist, but not angry enough to want to destroy the happiness she had apparently found in this unlikely place, no matter how short-lived it turned out to be. She could only envy her and pray for her future.

She turned her horse and kicked her into a trot, then a canter; she intended to be many miles away before dusk.

CHAPTER FOUR

Geoffrey returned to Winterton House that evening worse for drink, which always fuelled his temper. He should not have drunk so much, but he was angry. His latest conquest had proved to be a male whore, which he had not expected of one so young, and he was angry with him. He was also angry with his wife; it was not just that she had betrayed him so soon, but that she had betrayed him with his worst enemy.

He would never have admitted his reason for hating the Earl as he did, but in truth it had more to do with the man's attraction for women and his power over the entire neighbourhood than any harm he had suffered at his hands. Geoffrey always felt threatened by him and he knew he could cause him untold damage were he not a Papist with secrets of his own.

Geoffrey had married Julia for her fortune and to have a wife to hang off his arm at functions. People were beginning to talk about his single state; it was not normal for a man of means and title to remain unmarried for so long and her father was so desperate for an open door into society, she suited his purposes wonderfully well. He had expected her to obey him, as the church ordered, but obviously that would not happen. He saw her sneaking off that day to be with Summerville and to know she was expecting his bastard was just too much.

Now he must suffer the sight of her belly swelling and her breasts leaking, as well as having to pay out for midwives. They would have to be qualified midwives as well, or the gossips would start over again.

His threat had not been an empty one. As a man he had little compassion and he would not hesitate to smother the brat the minute it was born. He would make sure to be there, hovering in the next room like a good husband and he hoped it would look like its father; that would make it so much easier to carry out his intention.

But perhaps it was not too late to put a swift end to the life which grew within her, he thought viciously. He gripped the riding crop in his hand; he was looking forward to this. She would learn where her loyalties lie, even if she did have to learn the hard way.

He grabbed the banister rail on his way up the stairs to keep from falling and stopped for a moment to steady himself. The walls began to spin and he squeezed his eyes tight to stop the motion which was the result of too much strong wine.

He had been building up a rage throughout the day. He was too lenient with the whore last night, far too lenient. She deserved a beating and he was in the mood to deliver it.

He stood outside the door to her bedchamber for a few moments, once more trying to collect himself into some semblance of sobriety. He expected the door to be locked against him; it would be the sensible option and from what he had learned of his wife, she was no fool. But it opened easily and he flung it against the wall, his hands clenched into fists, then stopped when he realised she was not in her chamber.

"Julia!" He shouted as he hurried down the stairs and into the hall, then the sitting room.

One of the servants came running from the kitchens.

"Where is my wife?" Geoffrey demanded.

"I do not know, Sir Geoffrey," the woman replied. "I have not seen her all day."

He spun around and ran from the house to the stables. Darkness had fallen and there were no torches to light the stable area, so he had to go inside to see that Julia's mare was missing. His fury growing into a monster he could barely control, he went back inside the house to her bedchamber and found her jewel chest empty.

He stopped still, shaking his head as a sudden thought occurred to him. No, she would not have stolen his jewels, would she? Not the ones which had been in his family for generations. But his cabinet was empty, the lock on his jewel chest ripped open, and that was when he knew she had escaped and the monster finally consumed him.

He picked up the chest and flung it at the window, smashing the glass and leaving shards outside on the stones.

***

It was almost dark and Julia was exhausted when she first caught sight of the small farm house in the distance. She breathed a sigh of relief; she could not have ridden any farther and if the folk here were not kind, she would have to find a place to sleep outdoors. Guinevere was also weary and needed hay and water; surely they would be kind to her, if not to a married woman who had run away from her husband.

She thought about Geoffrey and his anger when he found her gone and for the first time she wondered if he would take the trouble to look for her. He had married for her fortune and for the credibility she would give him; he would look very foolish when it was learned his wife had left him after such a short time.

She also thought of the scene she had witnessed in the grounds of Summerville Hall. Poor Bethany; she was going to get her heart broken. Julia had no doubt about that, but was that not better than her own situation. At least she would know what real love was, something Julia would never experience.

She saw a light, the flame from a torch bobbing about in the gathering darkness as it moved toward her and her heart skipped. She could not see the person who carried it, only that it was a man, a tall, well built man from his silhouette, but she drew rein. She could not go another step and she was concerned for Guinevere. Still she stayed mounted, feeling safer lest this man posed a threat.

As the man came closer she saw that he had a kind face, dark auburn hair and beard and a ready smile.

"Good evening, Madam," he said. "Are you lost?"

"Sir, I am in need of shelter and my mare is in need of sustenance and rest."

He held out his free hand in a gesture for her to dismount which she did, but she was so stiff from the long hours in the saddle, she almost fell and he leapt forward to catch her.

"You are welcome," he said. "Let us get you inside. Your name?"

"Julia," she said. She did not want to tell him the rest.

"I am Charles Carlisle."

"This is your house?"

"It is, humble though it is. My father left it to me when he died." He swept his eyes over her expensive clothing, felt the satin of her gown against his fingers where he held her waist to assist her. "You are welcome," he repeated.

He began to lead the way towards the house, but she could not keep up with his brisk stride.

She was stiff and sore, muscles in her back screaming in agony. She stopped walking and clasped her stomach. She felt too stiff to move and for the first time the child inside her moved. She should have been overjoyed, but this was not the best entry into the world.

It was but a short distance to the house and as they walked Julia saw a few smaller cottages with lights coming from inside.

"My helpers," Charles said. "They have all gone to their homes for the night. There will be but the two of us in the house."

Any other time his words might have bothered her, but now they meant nothing. She was too desperate for a bed to lie her weary body on.

"Should I be concerned?" She asked.

"No. I only wanted you to know."

His smile was infectious and she soon found herself smiling back, despite her exhaustion and discomfort. The child moved again and this time her companion spoke.

"You are with child?" He asked.

Julia nodded.

"Will you still help me?"

In reply he passed the torch to her and tightened his grip around her waist.

"A woman with a babe in her womb does not run away from her home for no reason," he said. "That reason is her own affair, not mine."

Once inside the house, Charles guided her to a roughly made wooden chair and poured her some ale.

"I will see to your mare," he told her as he made his way outside.

While she waited, she saw a cookpot over the fire which was bubbling with a delicious aroma which made her realise how hungry she was. On his return, he ladled some onto a pewter plate and she sat with him at the small table. The food was a vegetable stew, no meat, but it was welcome. Everything was a far cry from what she was used to, a rough wooden square table with two benches, the rushes on the floor were plain with no flowers to improve their odour. In the corner of the room were two chairs and Julia could see another room in which there was a bed.

Should she feel uncomfortable, threatened by being alone here with a strange man? She had no idea but all she felt was comforted and relieved to be able to rest.

"You can sleep in there," he said after they had eaten. "I have a bed upstairs."

"You are very kind, Sir. Do you not want to know about me, why I am here alone?"

"Only if you want to tell me. But you are exhausted; tomorrow will do just as well."

***

His supper was almost cooked when Charles heard the sound of trotting hooves coming from the front yard. It was twilight and he was not expecting anyone and none of his tenants in the nearby cottages had mentioned an expected visitor.

He wiped his hands and peered from the small window to see the most beautiful woman, sitting side saddle upon a lovely little palomino mare. Charles had never seen anyone quite like her; her hair was almost white yet she was young and from the little he could see in the twilight, she appeared to be a lady of quality. What was she doing here? He wondered. Perhaps she had lost her way, but someone of her class should not be travelling alone. That thought was quickly followed by another; if she were here alone, perhaps her party had been set upon by robbers and she had managed to escape.

He grabbed a torch from one of the sconces on the wall and hurried outside, but stopped to admire her once more. Even in the fading light he could see how beautiful she was and he took note of the leather travelling bag she clutched across the front of her horse. He also noticed the wedding band she wore, solid gold and sparkling with tiny diamonds.

She looked exhausted and he decided to ask no questions. She was obviously in need of assistance and that he was happy to give her, even more so when her first thought was for her mare, not herself. It may well be the only thing he could give her, but he was sure it would be welcome.

***

Julia felt the chill as soon as she awoke. She kept her eyes closed for a few seconds, uncertain what she would see when she opened them. It was never cold like this at Winterton House, not with this icy bite making her nose and face so cold she could barely feel them. But when she opened her eyes, memories of the day before came back to her, the long journey on horseback, the empty roads through sparsely populated countryside, the fear that Geoffrey would be following behind her. She was more afraid of that than of any vagabond or robber on the road, which was foolish considering the fortune in jewels she carried with her.

She wondered if he had come home yet, if he had found his family jewels gone. She felt a flutter of guilt, but told herself firmly she deserved them. She had paid for them with bruises and tears.

She sat up in bed and pulled open the wooden shutter to see the landscape outside covered in snow which still fell in heavy flakes and settled on the ground.

There were people carrying straw and hay to the barns, carrying buckets of water. She had not seen any of this last night and she wondered if Guinevere was warm enough. The man who had given her shelter and fed her was nowhere to be seen, and she realised all at once she had trusted without question. Her glance flew to her travelling bag where Mr. Carlisle had placed it at the end of her bed. It was still there and as she looked into it, she felt guilty to have suspected him; the jewels were all still there.

She returned to the window where she saw him coming from one of the barns, his arms full of hay. Julia supposed there were animals here as it looked like a small farm or smallholding. She wondered what position the man named Charles held here, if he were a gentleman farmer of sorts, like Richard Summerville but on a very much smaller scale, or whether he was a tenant and this farm was the property of some other Lord of the Manor.

The farmhouse was sparsely furnished, the walls some sort of wattle and daub and the stairs unvarnished wood. The mattress on which she had slept was straw and it lay upon a bedframe of unplaned wood. No, this man was no gentleman farmer, just a kind man whom she was lucky to meet.

Thoughts of Richard brought back the memory of her sister in his arms and her heart skipped. She hoped she did not get hurt, but she could not worry about her now. She had to care about herself and her child; there was no one else to depend on, not this time. For the first time in her life she was alone, she had the responsibility of herself and a helpless babe. The idea was terrifying.

She had slept in her clothes last night. For one thing it was too cold to disrobe and for another she felt vulnerable alone in this house with a stranger. He was very handsome, and he had been very kind, but she was no judge of character. How could she be when she had led such a sheltered life? Her father had kept both her and Bethany close; they never went anywhere without chaperones and every function they attended had to be approved.

Now she sat on the edge of the bed and pulled on her boots, wrapped her fur cloak about her shoulders and went into the next room in search of her host. There was bread and cheese laid out as well as milk and some sort of ale and she was just wondering if it would be proper to help herself, when he came back into the house.

"You are awake," he remarked. "I hope you slept well. The bed is likely not what you are used to but you looked weary enough to sleep anywhere."

He gestured for her to sit and brought the food to the table.

"You are right," she replied as she ate. "I cannot recall ever being so tired. I do thank you for your hospitality. Is my mare well?"

"She is. She is in the stables with the work horses, warm and comfortable. I found her a rug, which is a little loose on such a fine lady, but better than nothing. Does she have a name?"

The question endeared him to her, as it meant he did not think of a horse as a mode of transport and nothing more.

"Guinevere," she replied.

He smiled.

"Ah. Is there an Arthur somewhere?"

Julia shook her head.

"She would more likely prefer a Lancelot I think," she murmured then she drew a deep breath to give herself courage, afraid her next words might change his kindness. "I have left my husband."

He only smiled.

"I guessed that was the case."

"Do you not want to know why?"

He reached out a hand and slipped the top of her sleeve down a little, revealing an old but vicious bruise on her upper arm. He had noticed it last night, when she removed her cloak to eat more comfortably.

"I think I know why," he said. "As I said before, I want to know only what you want to tell me."

"You seem to have enough on your hands with the snow and the animals. You do not need me causing you more trouble. If you can tell me where I can sell my jewels, I will go and leave you in peace."

"And then what? Do you have somewhere to go?"

She shook her head.

"Then stay here, as long as you can bear it. We are simple folk; we work hard for what little we have but what little we have we are happy to share with you. Your husband will not find you here, and if he does I am a very persuasive liar."

She looked at him sharply and was relieved to see the little grin playing about his mouth.

"Are you not concerned that I am depriving him of his child?"

He brushed gently at the top of her arm where the bruise still hurt.

"A man who would treat a beautiful woman like this, does not deserve her or her child."

CHAPTER FIVE

The house was not at all what Julia had been brought up to. The thatched roof was in constant need of repair; it seemed as soon as one hole was filled, another appeared. The furniture was mostly of rough wood, homemade by Charles and his helpers, the mattresses were of straw not the soft feather of her childhood and marriage.

After a few days the snow began to thaw and Julia once again broached the subject of the disposal of her jewels.

"I will take them into Norwich and see how much I can get for them. They all look very valuable to me, but I am no judge."

Julia pulled off her wedding band and dropped it into the bag with the other gems.

"Sell this as well," she said.

"Your wedding ring? Are you sure?"

"I would drop it in the well were it not worth a lot of hot meals. I want nothing to remind me of that man."

They sat at the table with the jewels before them, necklaces, brooches, rings, bracelets, all sparkling in the sunlight which streamed through the open shutters. Charles covered her hand with his own, reminding her of the same gesture Richard had made when they sat side by side on their mounts. Did all decent men feel only pity for her?

"You will not have to," Charles said now. "You can stay here as long as you like."

"What of your friends? Will they not disapprove of a woman running away from her husband?"

He shrugged.

"This is my house, my land. They are entitled to an opinion and I am entitled to require them to keep that opinion to themselves."

Charles made several journeys into Norwich and Bury to sell the jewels. He thought it would be less suspicious if he sold them one at a time and he knew his own limitations. He was a farmer and he looked like a farmer; his best hope was to pretend he found the gems on the road and to sell them in different places in small amounts.

He was astonished at the amount of silver coins he collected in exchange for such baubles. Why would anyone want to spend all that money on something to hang around a woman's neck, or dangle from her ears? He also thought like a farmer, and every piece he managed to sell saw him adding up how much fodder he could buy with it.

There was always lots of work to be done, animals to feed, sick animals to tend, sweeping and cleaning with water pumped from the well.

Laundry was done in the stream, once the snow cleared, and nobody called Julia 'My Lady'.

The floors were bare, the mattresses straw, the food poor but well cooked; there were no servants to do her bidding, no sumptuous gowns to enhance her figure, no one to brush her hair until it shone. But she had never been happier in her life.

Throughout her childhood she had felt she was nothing more to her parents than a commodity, something to be sold to assist them on the way to upper class circles. Her marriage had brought her nothing but fear, pain and disgust and the only person she had ever loved was her sister. Even her brother was distant, and treated both his sisters as property to raise him up in society. His own wife and Julia's mother were of a type, without opinions of their own, obedient wives who would follow their menfolk wherever they led them.

Now she was treated with respect by these people and it was not a false respect, given out of obligation for her social status. She had made friends, for the first time in her life, with some of the women from the cottages and Charles seemed to hold her in high regard. She had never known such deference from a man before. Even Richard, although he had treated her well, had never made her feel important as this man did.

As her figure swelled, people began to look at her curiously, but they asked no questions. She had no idea if that was Charles' doing, or whether people of the working class would have a different attitude to a pregnant woman travelling alone. She did not ask; she was happy for the first time in living memory, and she wanted nothing to spoil that.

Charles was a hardworking man and she found him funny and genuine, but he spoke of his own background only once.

"My father was a farmer," he told her. "He and my mother died in an outbreak of plague when I was sixteen. I had to sell off most of the farm as I could not manage alone. This is all that is left."

"So you own it?"

He had told her the first day, but Julia had never known a farmer who owned his land before. All the farmers she had ever known were tenants of some big estate and she thought they were all the same.

He shrugged.

"I do not think it was ever legally transferred to me, but I am the rightful heir, yes. The people here are made up of what was left of my father's workers and the odd straggler who has come along looking for work. They are loyal, that is the important thing."

"They are lovely people," Julia said. "I have never known people like this before, so open and forthright, never trying to keep up appearances. They remind me of my sister; she was always too outspoken for my father's taste, or indeed the taste of any of the men of our acquaintance."

"Where is she now?"

Julia smiled. She was still angry with Bethany, but she was pleased for her just the same.

"She married," she answered. "She married a man she could love. She was fortunate."

Charles grinned, glanced at his hands for a moment, then his eyes met hers.

"Strange," he said. "You come here dressed in satin and fur, with valuable jewels to sell. You ride in on an expensive mount. You have been raised from birth with fine things, with servants to do your bidding, with as good an education as a female can expect and you are accustomed to being Her Ladyship."

He paused and took her hand in his; she felt the callouses on his palm from hard work, not like Geoffrey's effeminately soft hand which she had felt only when there were people to impress. Not like Richard's hand either, his strong, but smooth hand, which had known nothing more strenuous than riding a horse and wielding a sword. But somehow this hand seemed more real; its touch even sent a little thrill along her spine.

"It must seem strange to you," she remarked.

"What seems strange is that you have had everything, yet I am the one who feels sympathy for you."

"Do you? I do not want your pity, Charles. I want your respect and your friendship, but not your pity."

"My friendship?" He moved to touch her face gently with his other calloused hand. "Nothing more?"

She laughed.

"Mr Carlisle, I am heavy with child."

"Really? I would not have noticed," he said with a laugh. "You have been generous with your money, but I hope you have enough to pay a midwife. It will not be long now, I think."

"Soon I will be a mother. I would like to stay here after the birth; I would like to raise my child among these good people."

"Those words are the ones I wanted to hear."

***

Charles found himself in a quandary. He had always been a decisive person, even when he was a child. He had never been confused about a decision; once his mind was made up he knew precisely where he was going and how to get there. The arrival of this beautiful woman had thrown his life into turmoil, his emotions into a terrifying mix of fear, love and compassion.

He had reached his twenties with no experience of women. He had never been in love, had never had more than a passing interest in a pretty face, but Julia invaded his dreams at night and his thoughts during the day. His heart skipped when he saw her, when he heard her sweet voice, and the sight of that ugly bruise on her shoulder sent his senses smouldering with the need to avenge her.

But she was not for him, was she? She had fled a brutal marriage, had come here in desperation and had seemed content to help as much as she could, but he did not expect it to last. She was a grand lady and the farm was a simple respite, a novelty to play with for a little while. She would soon become bored with the hard work and the poor surroundings; she might even decide it was worth her husband's harsh treatment to have her comforts back.

Charles could not afford to risk his heart by falling in love with her, but that is what was happening no matter how hard he tried to resist it.

***

Julia took on the tasks of cooking and sewing for everyone until she was able to do her part on the small farm. Unlike any other married woman, she knew almost to the day when her child would be due, as she knew to the very day when that child was conceived.

It was getting near the summer and she waited daily for a sign that the birth would soon happen. She was hot and uncomfortable and although the idea of giving birth in this poor place scared her, she also knew a little dart of excitement.

She had unpicked the stitching on the gowns she had brought with her and cut the fabric to make clothes for the baby.

"Will you not want to wear them again?" Charles had asked.

"No. Why would I? I am no longer Lady Winterton and I have no use for all this finery. I shall see if one of the women have anything I can wear after the birth."

"I will get some fabric next time I go to market, if you are sure."

"I am sure."

Charles went to the market and traded for some things she might need for the baby and on his return he wore a frown.

"What is it?" She asked. "You have had bad news."

"The King is dead," he replied. "Jane Grey has been proclaimed Queen."

"But that is good news. A Protestant Queen is what we wanted."

He sat beside her, took her hand affectionately and sent that little thrill through her heart once more. She had never known this sort of affection from a man; passion, but once, yes. Her swelling figure reminded her of that, but not real affection.

Julia was raised to know her duty. Despite being commoners, her wealthy father was determined his daughters would both achieve good marriages to allow him access to the upper circles of society. Neither of the girls had ever questioned that and Bethany had delighted her father by attracting the attention of an earl. Julia had never expected love from a marriage, even though it seemed her sister had found just that. She felt she could build a future with a man like this.

That was her main reason for keeping her child's parentage to herself. As long as Charles believed him to be her husband's son, there was no reason for him to know she was a whore, her child a bastard. She thought her heart would break if he were to discover the truth.

"We have never really talked about it, have we?" He said. "How fervent are your beliefs? How would you feel about a Catholic on the throne?"

"I cannot imagine such a thing," she replied, but her first thought was Bethany and her treacherous bargain.

"It might well happen," he told her. "Jane Grey will not sit securely on the throne. Mary Tudor will fight to reclaim it and she will be ruthless in her efforts to restore England to the Church of Rome."

"Let us pray you are wrong."

But he was not wrong. The reign of Queen Jane lasted little more than a week and while Julia gave birth to a son on the narrow, straw mattress in the little room she had grown accustomed to, Mary Tudor arrived in London with her army of soldiers and her chief advisors at her side. She promised religious tolerance, but the Protestants did not believe it and the Catholics did not approve of it.

The birth of Richard's son was very different to what she had been expecting when she had thought about motherhood, and very, very different from the way an Earl's son should arrive in the world.

There was no confinement chamber to which noble ladies would retire to await the birth, with their ladies. Nobody even suggested she should hide herself and she carried on as normal until the first pain came. She wondered if her sister had yet given birth; she wondered what she would think of this little room with its narrow, straw mattress.

"He is beautiful." Charles sat on the edge of the bed and gave his finger to the tiny hand of this newborn babe. "What will you call him?"

"Simon," she answered. He raised an enquiring eyebrow. "St Peter was called Simon before Jesus found him and told him he would be his rock. This child will be my rock, Charles. I love him so much already; do you think you can love him too?"

"I would be honoured."

As she held the tiny person in her arms she remembered Geoffrey's threat and could almost see him holding a cushion over the baby's face to smother him. She shivered with fear that he might be looking for her, that he might still find her and her son. She would kill him if he came near Simon and to hell with the consequences.

The women came in to see the new baby, all bearing gifts of clothes they had made for him and not one of them asked about his father.

It was but a few weeks before she regained her figure and Julia's next task was to make Charles Carlisle declare his love for her. She was certain he had that love. She was also certain that Charles keenly felt the great social divide between them and she wondered if perhaps she should be the one to say it first.

Her plan was put on hold when Charles told her, before she recovered from the birth, that the new Queen was busy putting in place her plans to reunite England with the Church of Rome. His words frightened her, but his next words shocked her into silence.

"She is aided by the Earl of Summerville," Charles told her. "His family have ever been fervent Catholics and he has been just waiting for this moment. Rumour has it he is as zealous as his Queen, that she keeps him close and values his advice above all others."

The Catholic Queen's right hand man? Her close adviser? Bethany had not bargained for that, Julia was certain. And if she had known, would it have made a difference? Would it have stopped her from marrying him? Somehow she doubted it.

Her memory showed her their childhood together, how they listened to the Protestant priests as they instilled into all three of the children the importance of their faith, how the Papist idolaters had corrupted Christ's message to suit themselves, how they grew rich on the terror of the place they called Purgatory, how they charged money in return for promises that they could shorten a soul's time there.

Her father hated all Catholics, and his children were supposed to do the same. But Bethany did not hesitate to promise to relinquish those beliefs when offered a title and the wealth which went with it.

Charles' tone was bitter, full of hatred for both the Queen and the Earl and for a moment Julia wondered if she should tell him that the man's wife was her own sister. Thank God he did not know that Simon was fathered by the Earl Charles so obviously despised. That was one secret she never wanted him to know.

She had never seen him angry before and she waited until she was sitting with her babe in her arms, her breast to his tiny mouth.

"Charles," she began. "The Earl; his Countess is my sister."

***

Julia stayed at the smallholding with Charles and his friends for the first few months of the new reign. She thought at first it would not affect her very much, as they were farmers, not close to the court as her sister was. How was she faring? Julia wondered.

She also wondered often just why His Lordship had chosen a commoner, inexperienced and many years his junior, to be his countess. She had no real knowledge of the nobility, she was too young to have very much to bring to the marriage and she was a Protestant. He knew that, and he likely thought her beliefs to be shallow if she would give them up so easily.

She imagined Richard would have wanted his wife at the palace for the coronation and the idea made her shudder. Was Bethany so far besotted with her new life and her new husband that she would have no qualms about meeting the Queen face to face?

Her attempts to get closer to Charles were thwarted by her revelation that her sister was the Countess of Summerville and she resented that. She knew she was falling in love with him; he was so kind and so good to all his people, a truly genuine man who she found very attractive. Sometimes she would lie awake and remember Richard Summerville's touch on her naked flesh and wish she could somehow persuade Charles to do the same.

It was but a few months before Charles was proved right about the Queen's religious intentions.

"I knew she was lying!" He declared. "I knew she would not allow religious tolerance. One of their mantras is that they shall not suffer a heretic to live. That is what they think we are, heretics."

She took his hand, held on to his arm.

Since recovering from Simon's birth, she had wanted very much to find a way into this man's heart. She was sure he cared for her and he treated the baby as his own, but she had been unable to tempt him to anything else. Perhaps the farming class had different rules; perhaps he thought her somehow above him, although she never used her title and would rather forget she had ever had it.

He filled her dreams at night, he filled her thoughts in the daylight, but he treated her as a much loved sister, not as the desirable woman she wanted to be to him.

What would her father think of that? He had fought so hard to find her a title, and she had discarded it for a farmer. She smiled at the thought.

"I am sorry, Charles," she said. "What can we do?"

He turned and smiled at her.

"What can we do?" He repeated. "That is what endears you to me; always you look to help."

"Can I help? Is there anything I can do to help?"

He looked at her thoughtfully for a few moments. It was a warm day and they stood outside in the front yard, the baby in his crib in the shade of the house. It was a comfortable scene, and one anyone would think of as a happy one, but Charles could not feel that way.

At last he spoke.

"You have discarded your status," he said. "You work with the animals like the others, you cook for us and sew for us and never once hanker after your wealth. I have to wonder when the novelty will wear off."

Quick tears filled her eyes and she released his arm and took a step away from him.

"What exactly do you mean by that, Sir?" She asked in a quivering voice.

She had been happy here these few months and while she was thinking she could learn to love this man, he was thinking she was playing some upper class game? She was hurt and that hurt was rapidly turning to anger.

"I mean, Julia, that you must miss the life you left behind. You were wealthy, titled, with fine clothes. Your husband was a brute who did not deserve you, but still this is not what you are used to, is it? It is not what you were raised for."

"What has that to do with anything?" She demanded angrily. "I came here seeking help for a terrible predicament; I thought I had found happiness, friendship, perhaps something more. But all the time you thought me playing at being a farmer, that I would soon want to return to the life I knew before." She turned away from him, folded her arms and swallowed back a sob. "You do not have to tolerate my presence any longer. I shall leave at first light."

She felt his hand on her arm as he came up behind her and turned her to face him. He ran his fingers through her thick, pale hair and turned her face to look at him.

"Something more?" He asked.

"It is of no matter."

"You are really happy here?"

"I was."

"Forgive me," he said. "I wanted to know where I stood. Since the evening I saw you riding towards my house I have been slowly falling in love with you. I have been afraid of that, afraid that you would grow weary of this life and want to return to your husband and his wealth. Are you really saying you would rather stay here with me?"

"Why would I want to return to him? You saw what he did to me."

"I have no knowledge of how the wealthy live, or their values. You tell me your sister married the Papist Earl for his wealth, despite having to give up her beliefs, despite even having to tolerate his infidelities. How was I to know you would not believe any sort of treatment worth the wealth?"

She stared up at him, her mouth turned down bitterly and hoping she could hold on to those threatening tears.

"I am not my sister, Sir," she said at last. "I have been happier here with you these months than ever in my entire life before."

She was rewarded with a delighted smile and he bent his head and kissed her, a long, tender kiss which she had only imagined all these months.

"So it is safe to fall in love with you?" He asked.

"Very safe."

He took her hand and led her inside the house, up the narrow, wooden staircase to the room above where he slept alone in a much larger bed. The mattress was straw, like the one downstairs, but it was thicker and now they stood beside that bed and he began to undress her.

Her memory showed her quick flashes of the only other time a man had undressed her like this. That time they had stood before an expensive, carved bed with soft feather mattresses and pillows and all around her were valuable furnishings, oak panelling and old paintings. She wondered if she would feel the same, or if her one afternoon with the Earl had somehow spoilt her for other men.

"I cannot offer you marriage," Charles said softly. "You already have a husband and what I am offering you is against the laws of man and church. You have only to say and I will leave you be."

How odd; before he bedded her, Richard had told her what he could not offer her. She began to wonder if there was anything a man could offer her, but she already knew the answer.

In reply she untied the front of his shirt and put her hand inside to gently caress his chest.

"Will you promise not to think badly of me?"

"I promise."

"Then it is right."

"It was not so very long ago the church had nothing to do with marriage," he told her. "A man and woman simply moved in together and they were wed in the eyes of the law."

"Then we, too, are wed."

He pulled her to him and kissed her again, then his hands trailed down her neck to her shoulders to slide her shift from her body and let it fall to the floor. She stood naked before him and he stirred as he had never stirred before, his lips touched her neck and his hand cupped her breast. She pulled the tie on his breeches and pulled him onto the bed, ran her fingers over his body while he gently stroked her flesh.

"I love you, Charles," she whispered against his neck. "I have never said that to any man before; I have never felt it for any man before."

"And I love you."

He gathered her close to him and she felt him inside her. It was like no other feeling she had ever had. Richard Summerville had made her feel like a woman again; this man made her feel like a woman who was loved and that meant everything.

CHAPTER SIX

Baby Simon was but a few weeks old when they were discovered. Julia was out beside the stream, some half mile away from the house, helping the other women with the laundry and washing the baby's clothes to be dried while the sun still shone.

Charles was watching the baby in the front yard. He had laid a blanket out on the grass for him to catch some warmth and he laughed at the child's efforts to roll over. Now he turned his head as a man approached on a big bay stallion. He had no idea who he was, but his clothing was rich and his expression was threatening. Charles scooped the child up into his arms and took him inside the house, laid him down in the crib he had made specially for him.

He returned to greet the visitor.

"I have come in search of my wife," the man said.

"Your wife, Sir? We have no strangers here."

"Do not waste my time," he replied. He pulled from his pocket a huge, blue stone set into a pendant and held it out. "The thieving whore had someone sell this to a broker in Norwich. Luckily for me, it is a well known piece and had she looked well enough she would have seen the engraving. The broker returned it to me, along with the name of the man from whom he bought it. Seems he recognised him; from there it took little effort to discover this place."

Charles silently cursed himself for a fool. Why had he not looked closely for identifying marks on such a valuable jewel? Perhaps because he had never had one in his hand before.

"Just tell me where my wife is and I will not press charges."

Now Charles was too angry to be afraid of arrest. He had fallen in love with Julia and when he thought of her beautiful body covered in fading bruises from this man's savagery, he wanted to pull him down from his horse and beat his superior face into the mud.

"Why do you want her?" He demanded. "You do not care for her; that is obvious."

Geoffrey raised an eyebrow.

"Why? Because she belongs to me, that is why. Because she is as much my property as this gemstone, and the other jewels she stole. Why do you protect her?" The sound of a crying baby from inside the house caused him to cast his eyes toward the building. He smirked. "I see the whore has given birth to Summerville's bastard."

Charles' eyes opened wide and he flinched, but said nothing. He had no wish to give this man ammunition to use against Julia, but if the baby was the son of the arch Papist, why had she not told him? Well, she had her reasons and he would keep his counsel. But for now, he had to get rid of this man before he ruined them all.

"Julia is no longer here, Sir," Charles replied. "That child you are referring to is my son."

"Your son?"

"Yes. I did sell the jewel, I admit it, but then Lady Winterton left as she did not want to involve us in her troubles."

Geoffrey laughed loudly, as though enjoying a good joke.

"You are a liar," he replied. "So, she is whoring with the peasant classes now. Why does that not surprise me? Who is your Lord? Where should I go to report the adultery to him?"

"I am no peasant, Sir. This farm is mine."

"Oh, excuse me." Geoffrey said mockingly, with a cruel smile, a smile his wife would recognise. "I will be back," he said. "You can keep the brat, but I want my property. I intend to have her publicly flogged for her adultery and you with her if you do not give her up. You may not find her so appealing when all that gorgeous hair is lying about her feet and she has a scarlet S painted on her hairless dome. You may not stir for her when she is stripped naked from the waist up in the market square with you beside her." He turned his horse and began to ride slowly away. "The choice is yours. You have until this hour tomorrow to decide."

***

Julia stood rigidly beside the stream, a basket containing her wet laundry balanced on her hip, her eyes open wide and her heart racing with fear. She knew that horse, she knew the figure of the man who sat upon him and terror twisted her gut until she thought she might vomit.

Geoffrey had found her. She was half surprised he would bother to look, to take time out of his busy schedule of pleasures to seek her out, but he likely wanted his jewels back. How did he find her? Was there no escape? And what was he telling Charles? Her husband knew who had sired her son, a fact she wanted to keep from her lover for fear it would be too much, for fear he would think her a whore.

She watched him turn his stallion and ride away then she hurried to the house, saw Charles disappear inside where baby Simon was crying and when she followed him she saw him pacing the floor with the babe in his arms, trying to soothe his tears. He kissed the child's cheek then put him into the crib and continued to rock it gently.

Did that mean Geoffrey had not told him, that he did not know the truth? Or could she hope that it did not matter? She would not ask, would not tempt fate. She would wait until he mentioned it himself.

Charles turned when he had put the child in his crib and met her with a smile, saw the fear in her eyes.

"You saw?" He asked.

She nodded.

"How did he find us?" She asked tearfully. "How could he have found us?"

"It was my fault," he answered as he took a step to stand before her and, setting the basket of wet clothes on the floor, pulled her into his arms. "One of those jewels had engravings on which led the jeweller to him. I am so sorry."

Julia clung to him, feeling her happy interlude coming to a close, her hopes for the future crumbling.

"I will have to leave. I shudder to think what he will do."

Charles was not about to pass on the threat Winterton had made; he saw no point to scaring her further.

"We will leave," he said. "Together."

"Where? Where will we go? This is your home, your property. I cannot ask you to give it all up for me."

He pulled her close to him, kissed her longingly, ran his hand gently through her thick, blonde hair and sighed softly.

"I would give up anything for you," he said. "I have waited my whole life for you to come along and teach me about love; I am not about to give you up to that monstrosity of a man who has the barefaced gall to call you his wife."

They packed as many of their belongings as they could into a wooden cart with an open bed, hitched up to one of the workhorses. Guinevere was tied to the side so they could keep an eye on her, Julia held the baby in her lap, and they said goodbye to all the people she had come to call 'friends'.

"You can have the place," Charles told them. "Do what you can with it. It is yours, but we cannot stay. It is too dangerous."

Nobody asked any questions; they all trusted Charles to know what was best and now they would have to fend for themselves.

"Where are we going?" Julia asked as they rode away.

Charles shrugged.

"Who knows? Anywhere is safer than here, even if we have to camp out in the forest like Robin Hood."

She snuggled against him. She would never have believed the prospect of driving into the unknown would not scare her half to death, especially with a small baby to care for. She felt safe with Charles, no matter what.

They drove for about three hours, stopping in a forest clearing to feed the infant and getting closer to the coast. Eventually they came to a manor house, a large, brick built building with smaller cottages around it. It was the sort of place an important man might own, but the whole place seemed deserted.

The fields were overgrown, the grass far too long to be of any use as grazing and it seemed obvious no horse or cattle had touched these fields in a very long time. No one had tended either the crops or the buildings themselves, but it was a rich land, a wealthy, if moderate house.

He climbed down from the cart and made his way cautiously toward the house. It was getting late, dusk was drawing in and they had both had a tiring and terrifying day. He desperately hoped this place was as deserted as it seemed, that it would be somewhere they could stay, if only for tonight, for Julia to rest and be safe.

He pushed the front door, expecting it to be locked but it moved inward. Charles turned to see that Julia had put the baby in his crib aboard the cart and climbed down to follow him. He pushed the door further. Everything was silent; even the birds seemed not to want to sing and as he stepped inside he saw this was indeed a wealthy house.

The furnishings were not extravagant, but definitely more than he could afford; there were oak settles and embroidered cushions and a long table of the kind an important man would sit at the head of. Everything was covered in a thick layer of dust, proving this place had not been inhabited in many months.

It was not long before the smell caught up with them, a ghastly stench of rotten meat and Charles tried to take a step back but Julia was behind him now and he collided with her. She held on to his shirt as she followed him inside. Then she screamed. Hanging from a beam beside the staircase was the body of a man, dressed in a black velvet suit and a silk shirt with lace at the cuffs.

Julia held her hand against her mouth to protect it from the stench of putrid flesh emanating from the hanging man. She turned and ran outside to breathe in the fresh air in gulping lungfuls.

Charles followed and gathered her into his arms.

"What do you think happened to him?" Julia asked in a frightened whisper.

"It seems he hanged himself, which is a mortal sin."

"I wonder why. It seems likely he was all alone here, no servants even. Why else would his body still be hanging, rotting away like that in an abandoned house?"

"The little cottage next to the house is the kitchen, I think. You could see about finding some supper while I cut him down and bury him. Perhaps we can stay in one of those small cottages for tonight and tomorrow we can clean the house. If nobody else wants it, why should it not be ours?"

For the first time that day, hope touched her heart and she smiled.

"It is almost the same as Winterton House, only older."

Then she remembered the writing carved into the stone archway under which they had passed. She had not noticed before, she was too tired and too concerned about their immediate future, but now she ran back to the gates and stood outside, staring up at the name above them.

"What does it say?" Charles asked, hurrying toward her.

"It is the name of the house," she replied. "Sinclair Manor."

***

Geoffrey set out the next day clutching an arrest warrant in his hand and accompanied by soldiers sent by the county mayor to aid in his quest. He was still furiously angry, could not wait to get his adulterous wife in the market square for the whipping she deserved. It was all there on the warrant, signed by the mayor, a public whipping.

He wished he could shave that hair himself; it would give him a great deal of satisfaction to know that her greatest beauty was lying at her feet, that she would be attracting no more lovers with it. It would take years to grow again, years he did not intend to be easy. But it would be more humiliating for the bailiff to do it; that would be better for her.

He hoped the peasant farmer she was whoring with would give her up. He had no qualms about extending the warrant to him, as that was the law, but he would rather the whole county did not find out that his wife had run away with a peasant.

Good thing he had not found her before the brat was born. She would have evaded her proper punishment if she were with child. Memory of the child reminded him of its father and he realised he had forgotten him. He would have to go about this business very stealthily until the actual flogging took place. If Summerville got to hear of it, he would interfere, there was no doubt of that. He would do it for her sister if nothing else.

He put the blue gem back into his cabinet before he left. He had some silver coins with him, which he intended to use to pay off the farmer lover so that he would give her up, which he was sure he would. What else could one expect of a man of his class?

As he rode into the courtyard he looked about at the surrounding land. It was deserted except for a woman who was washing in the stream. He dismounted and went inside the house, knowing at once that it was just as uninhabited.

They had gone, all their belongings had vanished and the place had an eerie feeling of emptiness about it. Outside in the stables he found no sign of any horses; he walked across the yard to where the soldiers stood waiting, furious that they would know he could not keep his own wife from eloping with such a man. Furious, too, that this peasant had the audacity to defy him! He did not expect this; it never once occurred to him that the man would give up everything he had to protect a slut like Julia.

Perhaps he had not given it all up, Geoffrey thought suddenly. Perhaps he was only waiting for them to leave before he returned. He called to one of the soldiers.

"You, stay here. Stay here and wait lest they return. Where else do they have to go? They will be back and when they are you are to arrest Lady Winterton on a charge of adultery and theft. Do you understand?"

***

They buried the corpse in the little cemetery which seemed to be attached to the house. It was full of people named Sinclair according to the many tombstones, so Charles and Julia simply assumed he was one of them. Who else would be in a position to commit suicide in the manor house?

"Do you think it is right?" Julia asked. "To bury him in consecrated ground like this?"

"Where else?" Charles answered with a shrug. "If we send for the village priest questions will be asked and this poor soul will be buried at a cross roads somewhere. He must have been desperate to take his own life; I'll not be the one to condemn his soul as well."

There was quite a bit of land surrounding the manor house and Charles got to work making it arable again, but not for the first few weeks. They could hardly settle, knowing it was not theirs, that they did not belong. Someone could easily come along and claim it.

They would wait and while they waited they explored the house and found in a chest in the attics, books and writings by the great reformers. Martin Luther's books were all there, as were those of John Calvin.

"So they were Protestants," Julia remarked, holding on to his arm. "I wonder what happened to them. Do you think they were all arrested?"

"It is likely, being as they all vanished. But what of the body we found? Perhaps he was away somewhere and could not bear the emptiness. We will likely never know."

But his assumption was wrong. Only the following morning a man appeared in the courtyard, on foot, and was seen from the window.

"It seems we have company," Charles remarked unnecessarily. "We may have to move on."

Julia lifted little Simon into her arms to protect him. He was crawling now and did not like his freedom curbed. He squirmed about in her arms, wanting to get down and he was getting too heavy for her.

"Shush now, Simon," she said softly. "You can get down in a minute, when this gentleman has gone."

Charles went outside to meet the visitor.

"Ah," the stranger began. "I thought I saw signs of occupation. I half hoped one of the family had escaped and returned, but it was a forlorn hope."

"Escaped?"

He made no reply but held out a hand in greeting.

"Jacob Barnes is my name, Sir," he said. "I live in the smaller manor just over the way."

He pointed across two fields to another house, this one smaller than Sinclair Manor and with a thatched roof. Charles shook his hand warily.

"Charles Carlisle," he replied.

"Well, Mr Carlisle, I am very pleased to meet you. This place has been going to ruin since the Sinclairs met their fate. God alone knows what happened to Elliot."

"Elliot?"

"Their son. He was the only survivor."

Charles felt sure the man of whom his visitor spoke must be the one he had buried in the Sinclair cemetery, but he said nothing. He was wary of revealing too much to this stranger. He and Julia were criminals in the eyes of the law; she had deserted her marriage and committed adultery, a crime in itself, and she had stolen his jewellery. Charles had sold it. They were both wanted by the authorities and then there were the Protestant writings they had found. How was he to discover where this man's allegiance lay without giving himself away?

The two men eyed each other suspiciously for a few moments, neither wanting to speak and risk giving themselves away. The awkwardness between them would have lingered much longer had Julia not interrupted them.

She carried her son outside, hoping the child's presence might give the two men something insignificant to talk about. Charles turned and took the child from her.

"My wife," he introduced her. "And my son, Simon."

Julia felt a little thrill as he spoke those words. He had never called her his wife before and now he was claiming Simon as his son. A wave of joy rushed over her; she cared nothing that they were homeless, that they were fugitives, forced to pray in secret, only that the man she loved had accepted her and her child. She was very glad she had never told him who the boy's father really was.

"Handsome boy," Jacob remarked.

"Will you not take some refreshment, Sir?" Julia asked.

Jacob was thoughtful for a few moments, then at last he drew a deep breath and let it out in a heavy sigh.

"I will come to the point, Mr Carlisle," he said. "I came to see if Elliot had returned or sobered from whatever drunken stupor God had condemned him to. I did not expect to find strangers here, but if Elliot is not here, nobody else has a claim. You can stay; I'll not be the one to deter you."

Charles made up his mind at last.

"Please, come inside," he said and led the way into the house, where he gestured his guest to a seat while Julia poured ale from the cask they had found in the cellar.

Jacob looked around at the cobwebs still hanging from the corners of the room. Julia had dusted the surfaces, but saw no point in doing too much until a decision about their continued residence had been made.

"When we arrived a couple of days ago," Charles said at last, "we found the corpse of a young man hanging from the rafters. I can only assume that was Elliot Sinclair."

Jacob's eyes widened in shock, but Charles noticed he made no move to cross himself. Did that mean he was a Protestant? Did that mean they could speak freely?

"Suicide?" Jacob said.

"It certainly seemed so."

"The body?"

"We buried him, in the little cemetery. We gave him a service."

Jacob began to laugh, while Charles and Julia exchanged a glance and a frown.

"That cemetery was consecrated to the Protestant faith," he said. "I found that ironic."

"Why?"

"Where do your loyalties lie, Mr Carlisle? Please, be honest with me. We cannot skirt around each other forever."

Charles once more exchanged a glance with Julia.

"You first," he said.

"I am Protestant. I shall deny it if you repeat that, say you are lying to get my lands."

Charles smiled, Julia too.

"That is a relief, Sir. We found some books in the attics which told us the Sinclairs were Protestant and we used Cranmer's book for the funeral service. We would not have known how to do anything else."

Jacob shifted in his seat a little.

"Elliott Sinclair betrayed his entire family to the Catholic church. They were all executed, burned at Smithfield. They had no idea their son was a secret Papist. That is why I found it ironic that you should have given him a Protestant burial in a Protestant cemetery."

CHAPTER SEVEN

Charles and Julia learned that Jacob and his family were devout Protestants and were holding services and lessons in their house. They also learned that Sinclair Manor had been a hub for escaping Protestants until they were betrayed.

Some women arrived to help Julia to clean the house and they felt they had been accepted, especially when Jacob told them about the family chapel inside the house where Lord Sinclair had held Protestant services.

They would never have found it on their own. It was hidden behind a bookcase which slid along the wall to reveal a chapel, big enough to hold about twenty or thirty worshippers. The chapel was bare of any statues and idols, the Bible which stood on the stand was in English, one of the copies commissioned by King Henry VIII and now outlawed. Hundreds of these Bibles had been burned already since that King's daughter took the throne; this one was rare and precious.

"Are you happy with this?"

Charles had just said goodbye to the neighbour and told him they would be willing to allow Protestant services and lessons in the chapel. The books they had found were the ones

Lord Sinclair himself had used to teach the neighbouring families.

"It is a little late to ask me now," she replied.

He pulled her into his arms, kissed her.

"Forgive me," he said. "I am unaccustomed to pleasing anyone other than myself. I am ashamed to say I forgot that I am now a married man."

She smiled, her smile lighting up her beautiful face and making his heart skip with joy. She slipped her hand inside his shirt and stroked his nipple.

"After last night?" She said. "You have forgotten you are a married man, after last night?"

How could he have forgotten last night? They had made love in the huge, feather bed with its carvings and canopies, its bedcurtains to shut out the cold. They had climbed together to heights of ecstasy and did it all again. God how he loved this woman, how fortunate he felt himself that she had chosen his farm to ride into when she needed help.

He laughed then held her tight. Despite the danger, he had never been so happy.

"Well?" He said. "If you feel threatened, if you are not happy about it I will tell Jacob at once that we will have no part in it."

"No. It is right that we should do our part and we should do our part to help the Protestants escape to France."

"That is very dangerous."

"But it has to be done. We have space here; we can hide escaping Protestants, just as Lord Sinclair did. We can pretend they are servants or something, and we can use the cart to get them to the coast as well as the Sinclair carriage if we paint over the crest on the doors. Until we can find some way to get rid of the evil witch who sits on the throne, it is all we can do."

So Sinclair Manor once again became a sanctuary for loyal Protestants. It seemed Lord Sinclair had spent a lot of money on adapting his house, putting in secret spaces in case of interference from the Queen's soldiers or the bishops. It seemed a fitting tribute that his work should be revived.

"Elliot will be turning in his grave," Jacob remarked. "Damn good thing, too."

***

They heard news from London from time to time, about the latest schemes of the Queen and her advisors to trap loyal Protestants and the more they heard, the more shame Julia felt that the man she had spent one passionate afternoon with, the man who had fathered her son, was the hated overlord of the carnage.

Simon was growing fast, and the faster he grew the more like that overload he looked. Charles had seen Lord Summerville once when they hid from a party of soldiers on their way to the ships, but he had made no mention of the resemblance. Likely it would not occur to him that the Earl could possibly be Simon's father; likely he only thought he reminded him of someone. At least she hoped so.

But she occasionally thought fondly of that afternoon, of the kindness she had received at Richard's hands, of the passion she had felt, and she found it very hard to believe the stories about him. And what of Bethany? She had made this bargain, knowing he was Catholic, she had even agreed to follow him, but she had not expected this. She could have had no idea of his importance in court circles, in the Queen's circles.

Was Julia's naïve and outspoken sister now living at court, facing the Fanatic every day of her life? Was she agreeing with everything the Queen said and did because she adored her husband, or was she having to bite her ever liberal tongue and keep silent for his sake?

Julia looked about at her poor surroundings and knew she had been the more fortunate sister, even if they did have to keep vigilant lest Geoffrey should find her again. With this in mind, one of the small cottages was always ready for her and her son to hide quickly. It had a trapdoor leading down to a cellar which had been furnished comfortably by Lord Sinclair for his Protestant fugitives. There were also many tunnels and secret rooms in the manor house itself where she could disappear at a moment's notice.

She was in the courtyard when she heard the sound of horses approaching and she picked up the little boy and carried him inside the cottage, took him into the second room and began to brush the straw away from the trapdoor, ready to escape. She opened the wooden shutter a fraction of an inch, just enough to glance from the tiny window, and saw Charles running across to the cottage to make sure she was safe inside, but she stopped what she was doing when she saw who rode the lovely chestnut mare, when she saw the beautiful riding gown, the matching hat with its sweeping feather, the dark hair and smooth face.

Wealth oozed from this fine figure of a woman, wealth and status bought with her soul. Julia felt the anger rising as she stayed where she was and listened as Charles greeted her sister, his arms folded, his manner hostile.

Bethany must have had her reasons for coming here. Julia had fled without a word to her; she had likely been worried about her all this time and for that Julia was grateful. It was best to get it over with, to face her and assure her she was safe and happy. That was the only way she would have peace of mind and stay away.

What would happen if His Lordship decided to follow her here? They would all be doomed, arrested and charged with heresy.

"It is all right, Charles," she said as she stepped outside the cottage.

"We cannot trust her. Think to whom she is wed."

Julia sighed wearily, wishing Bethany had not come, had not been able to find her. If she could find them, so could her husband and she had to believe she would say nothing to him about their whereabouts. Did she even realise the danger? Julia was uncertain, but it was too late to hide now.

"She is my sister, Charles," she assured him. "She will not betray us."

Why was she so certain of that? Her memory showed her the last time she had seen Bethany, clutched in the arms of her husband. That she loved him had never been in doubt, but could Julia trust her? Unless he had changed her completely, she could be relied on to keep quiet.

She dismounted and followed Julia into the tiny cottage, while Charles took away her servants to give them refreshments.

"Why have you come here?" Julia demanded. "How did you find me?"

"Anthony had some word from people Richard knows. I have told no one, I swear it. I never would, you must know that."

Julia nodded.

"I hope you are right," she said. "If you can find me, so can Geoffrey."

"Why would he want to?" Bethany said, that naivety showing again, despite everything. "From what I saw, he has little use for a beautiful woman."

"Never mind," Julia said, not wanting to talk about her husband. "Why have you come?"

"I came to be sure you are safe, nothing more."

That is when Simon appeared from the other room and stood in the doorway gazing up at the two women. To deny his parentage was pointless; he looked more like his father every day.

"So this is Richard's son?"

Julia could not help but notice the catch in her voice as she asked the question. It must be hard for her, knowing the man she loved had fathered a son on her sister.

"Now do you see why I wanted you to refuse him?" She said. "Once you accepted him I could not ask for his help."

"You mean he does not know he has a son?"

"No, and you must promise not to tell him."

"Is it likely that I would?" Bethany replied, biting her lips to keep them from creasing.

"You have seen me now," Julia said. "As you can see, I am well. I am with Charles now."

"What did he mean about knowing to whom I am wed?"

Julia was astonished. Could it be possible that her sister really did not know the importance of her husband in Mary's court? Was she being ingenuous or was she really that naïve still?

"It is not important," she replied. "Just believe that I love Charles; he has taken me and my son and will care for us as best he can. I will say no more. You cannot expect either one of us to trust the wife of the most feared and hated man in England."

Bethany stepped back, looking shattered by her words.

"Richard?" She whispered. "Do you mean Richard?"

"Of course. He is at the right hand of the fanatic. He will be helping her devise ways to trap loyal Protestants and send them to the stake. That is what he does, Bethany. Are you saying you did not know?"

She was shaking her head slowly, looking utterly bewildered.

"You are wrong," she insisted. "He would never do such a thing. He is trying to make her curb her enthusiasm, trying to make her convert the Protestants peacefully."

"I am glad to hear you call us Protestants and not heretics at least. It shows he has not managed to corrupt you completely."

"He has not corrupted me at all."

"You knew he was Catholic when you married him. You were prepared to turn for his wealth."

Bethany took a deep breath and swallowed.

"I cannot deny it. Just as you knew what he was when you let him take you to his bed."

"It was one afternoon of comfort, Bethany, that is all," she answered with a weary sigh. "I did not promise to join the papists and idolaters in exchange for his wealth. Now you know how Judas Iscariot must have felt when he realised what he had done for his thirty pieces of silver."

Julia regretted her words as soon as she saw the hurt behind the tears in her sister's eyes. She really had no idea what her husband was; she believed her own lies. Bethany spun around and fled the cottage, called for her servants as she mounted her pony and rode away, leaving Julia to wonder how she could have used such harsh words to someone she had once loved.

And she wondered what Bethany would do now, if she would confront His Lordship and in so doing give away the hiding place she and Charles had carefully preserved. She cursed herself for losing her temper, for allowing her emotions to guide her tongue.

Bethany loved Richard, she trusted him; it was possible she would not see the danger, that she would tell him everything and then they would all be ruined. Damn!

"We will just have to be extra vigilant," Charles said when she voiced her fears. "This place is ideal for our work; it would be a terrible shame to have to give it up and what are the chances of finding another abandoned house out of which to work?"

"Charles, I am so sorry. I am such a fool."

He took her cheek in his rough hand and leaned down to kiss her.

"No, you are no fool. And if you are not, I can only hope that neither is she. We have work to do, many more people needing our help to get to the coast tonight and I cannot think what this means."

He held out a piece of parchment upon which was written a warning, a message to stay away from Felixstowe tonight, to take the refugees to Yarmouth instead.

She gave him a puzzled frown.

"Where did it come from?"

He shook his head.

"It was attached to the door with an arrow this morning," he said. "I had no chance to show it to you before because your sister arrived. It is unsigned; it could be some sort of trap to make us reveal ourselves."

"Or it could be someone in the know wanting to help," she said.

"We will not know which until we test it. Tonight, we leave from Felixstowe, as planned.

It is too late to change it, but we will watch carefully to see how the land lies."

That night the escaping Protestants and their escorts, armed with crossbows and hastily made longbows, watched for hours as soldiers searched the harbour. So it was true; they had a friend at court. Charles' mind wandered back to that morning when Lady Summerville had arrived to claim her sister and he could think of no other who would have done this. Surely she was the only one who knew their whereabouts and also had knowledge of the Queen's plans, of Richard Summerville's plans. If he was right, and he prayed he was, it would mean she would say nothing about their hiding place and he and his beloved Julia were safe.

They had missed the tide by the time the soldiers gave up and left and would have to return tomorrow, but at least they were all alive.

***

During the next weeks, Julia wished more than once that she had not been quite so harsh with Bethany. She loved the man and Julia could well understand that; it must have come as a terrific shock to learn what he really was. She did not seem surprised about Simon though.

Julia recalled the Christmas she had met Lord Summerville, how she must have acted strangely in Bethany's eyes. Perhaps she had realised she was with child, perhaps Geoffrey had told her and she would know it was not fathered by him. She had known all along, had she not? She had known her own husband was the father of her sister's child, but still she had come looking for her, come to ensure her safety. And all she had got in return were bitter words and contempt.

Many more Protestants were being helped out of the country by Charles. They came to the house as field hands and servants and left under cover of darkness for a dangerous journey across the channel to a foreign land whose King could turn on them at any time. Julia sighed heavily; what was the point? When would the damned Papist hag die and leave England in peace?

The Queen had twice announced herself with child, striking fear into the hearts of the Protestants who could not contemplate no end to the terror through a Catholic heir. Each time was false; the woman was too old to bear a child, but still she lived, still faithful Protestants were not safe in their homes.

Although Julia could have no idea then, for her it would be over sooner than she wanted. She had found happiness with Charles, even though the work was hard and her once soft hands were calloused. She would have loved to withdraw from the work of helping Protestants, live quietly on their farm and do nothing but work the land and love each other, but Charles would not do that. He was right, of course. The work was important, he was important in the cause and it was her place to help him.

"I will keep you out of it," he said. "If that is your wish, I will remove the whole headquarters somewhere else. I will think no less of you, I promise. You have Simon to consider."

They were sitting up in bed, preparing to sleep for a few hours before he rose and led his group of fleeing Protestants to the waiting ships. She shook her head.

"No, Charles. I am being silly; I just want this wretched Queen to die so we can have some peace with her sister on the throne."

"As do I," he replied. "But short of assassinating the woman, and that has failed before now, what else can we do but save as many as we can?"

He laid down and pulled her with him, to hold her against himself. He felt so fortunate to have found her; she was way above him in the social scale, but he felt sure she loved him as he loved her. She could have taken the proceeds from the sale of her jewels and gone far away to start a new life with her son, somewhere her brutal husband would never find her. But she had stayed; he could almost feel the love from her every time he held her in his arms, every time he felt her soft flesh against his, her heart beating against his own.

"I love you, wife," he said now as he slipped his hand inside her shift and caressed her breast.

"You are my wife, in the eyes of God and all that is right. You were never really wed to that deviant."

"I love you, too, more than I ever thought possible. I worry about you, when you go off with the refugees; each time you leave, I am afraid I will never see you again."

"I will not say it cannot happen, because it would be a lie. All we can do is pray for our safety and make the most of our time together."

He slipped her shift from her shoulders, releasing her breasts to his hands and his lips. He caressed her body, stroked his fingers over every inch of her until she gasped with bliss, and made love to her for the very last time.

CHAPTER EIGHT

As Mary's reign continued, more and more Protestants were desperate to flee the country and Charles found himself a leader among a system of subterfuge in order to get these people away. He did not ask for the task, but it seemed Sinclair Manor was an ideal place. Of course it was; Lord Sinclair had made sure of that and it had cost him his life and the lives of his family and servants. Charles felt somehow beholden to him and he felt the work he was doing was a tribute to his memory and the memories of his household of martyrs.

Jacob had told him all he knew of the family and their downfall, his eyes filling with hatred when he spoke of their treacherous son.

"He was betrothed," Jacob said. "I do not know for certain what happened to her, but she was not here when the soldiers came. I was told she escaped."

"I wonder if she knew what he was," Charles said.

"I doubt that very much. Lady Elizabeth came from a prominent Protestant family and I am quite sure she knew nothing of Elliot's beliefs, or his intention to betray them all."

"I assume he loved her then, since she was not betrayed with the others."

"I think he did in his way, but a lady like that would never have wanted to marry him after what he did. I heard she went home to her father and later married an Earl. A sweet lady, a very sweet lady. I pray for her happiness."

Although a farmer, Charles was educated, which made all the difference to the smooth running of the operation. Julia prepared food and purses of money for the refugees; it was the last of the money paid for Geoffrey's jewels and it would be hard when it ran out.

Charles and some of his followers drove the carts which took them to the coast. The warning letters continued to come, but he still had no clue as to who their friend at court might be. Despite what Julia had told him, he could think of no one but her sister who would be doing this for them.

That last night no warning came, so he believed it was safe. There were about twenty people altogether, including the helpers; more would attract too much attention and as it was most of them were hidden under bales of hay in the open bed of the cart.

When they arrived at the harbour, they were blocked by a man on horseback, his silhouette the only thing showing in the moonless night.

"You must go back!" A voice cried out. "It is a surprise attack. We had no time to warn you."

Was this the one? Had Charles finally found their saviour? He had no time to ask questions before the man turned his huge stallion and rode away, while Charles turned the cart around. That is when he felt the sudden sharp stab in his shoulder and cried out in pain. He had been shot.

***

With help from one of the other men, Julia managed to extract the musket ball from Charles' shoulder before he regained consciousness. She remembered from an injury she suffered in childhood how the physician had talked of infection and how important it was to keep the wound clean and she had tended to that with hot water and a little salt. Salt was too expensive to waste, but it was the best she could think of.

They could scarce afford a physician, even if it were not too dangerous to send for one. Such a person would want to know how Charles had got a ball stuck in his shoulder.

Charles' eyes flickered open slowly and his first thought was the tall silhouette on the tall horse. He looked around, wondered if he had dreamed him, but the pain in his shoulder as he tried to move assured him it was all real. Julia was also real, sitting on the bed beside him and bathing his forehead with a cool cloth.

He reach up and gripped her wrist, pulled her down to kiss her lips with his own.

"What happened?" He mumbled.

"You were shot."

"What with? It feels like a cannon wrenched through me."

"Stephen said the soldier carried an Arquebus. I managed to get the ball out, but you will be weak for a few days."

"And the people? Were they captured?"

She shook her head.

"You got them away in time. But we will have to try again tonight, before they are missed by their own neighbours."

He nodded, then tried to lift himself up but she pushed him down. She held a mug of water to his lips, wiped the spillage with the cloth. Strangely, she felt pleased to be doing these things for him and pleased he would not be risking his life again for a few nights at any rate.

"I will be better by tonight."

"No, you will not."

"But there is no one else. These people do not understand the route, the way to identify ourselves; they will get us all captured. I have to go."

"No," she insisted. "I will go."

"You cannot."

"Why? I am more than capable, Charles. You know that."

She was; she was likely more capable than he was himself but he was terrified of losing her. He did not want his beautiful Julia to risk her life for this or any cause; he would prefer that they all died than that she should put herself at risk. But he had little choice, so that night it was Julia who set out to lead the escaping Protestants to the waiting ships.

***

Simon's voice from downstairs woke Charles. Forgetting his injury, he tried to roll over but flinched with pain and flopped back onto his back as he came fully awake.

"Mama," the child was saying. "Where is Mama?"

"Hush, now, darling," a female voice replied. "You come with me lest you wake your papa."

Charles frowned, wondering where Julia was, then remembered she had led the refugees last night. Birdsong drew his attention to the obvious fact that it was daylight and Simon was asking for his mother. She had not returned.

Once again he tried to haul himself up, once more he tried to roll out of the bed, his heart hammering in panic and praying to God that he was still asleep and dreaming. But he had not the strength to move and the pain in his shoulder tore through him just as though he was being shot all over again.

A creak on the stair drew his attention and he prayed it was her, it was Julia returned at last. But no; it was Thomas, his friend who did not help with the evacuation, who was illiterate and incapable of displaying the sort of authority needed to get to the ships.

"Julia," Charles whispered hoarsely.

Thomas shook his head slowly.

"She has not returned," he mumbled. He went to the table and poured ale for Charles, took it to the bedside. "Nobody has returned."

Charles cursed this damned wound which would not allow him to get himself out of this bed. He had to go, he had to find her, find out what had happened.

"Help me up," he said, holding out his hand.

Thomas took it and pulled him into a sitting position, then steadied him as he swung his feet to the ground. Charles felt stiff from lying so long and giddy from the loss of blood and he closed his eyes for a moment, then reached out for his jacket. Thomas helped him put it on.

"Should you be getting up?" He asked. "Julia would not want you to get up."

"Julia is not here, is she?" Charles demanded, catching back the tears which were clear in his tone. "She is in danger and I need to find her."

"And what about Simon?"

This voice was a woman's, Emily who lived in one of the cottages, who had taken the little boy away and fed him while Charles was still waking up. He had not heard her tread on the creaky staircase; he was too worried and he hurt too much.

"You care for Simon," he replied. "You will? You will look after him for me?"

"I will, but you will not be back if you leave here still with that wound. You must let us help you recover and you must send someone else to learn the news."

She was right, damn it! He knew she was right but he could not bear to stay here, helpless, doing nothing while his beautiful wife was in so much danger. He did not trust anyone else to discover what had happened. How could he? Had there been anyone else capable he would have forbidden her to go at all and now all he could do was contemplate what life would be like without her.

She would be taken to prison, she would be interrogated, asked about the rest of the group, asked to betray them all and she would suffer untold horrors rather than do that. He recalled the tales he had heard about Anne Askew, the Protestant preacher who had been tortured till her limbs were dislocated and still she would not give them the answers they wanted.

He felt hot tears clouding his vision and wished they would all leave him alone so he could pray for her safety and weep for her loss.

***

"Go back!"

Julia heard the voice as the cart drew to the edge of the forest. They had come by the rough dirt track through trees for cover and were just emerging when the voice rang out. The voice was familiar, very familiar but Julia shook herself.

She knew at once who it was and assumed he was talking to his own men, but why would he be telling them to go back? It made no sense. All she knew was that these people were depending on her to get them to the ships tonight, before it was too late. If they were missed by their own neighbours, some of whom were ardent Catholics, they would be suspected and investigated.

She sat and waited for more voices, more warnings which may or may not be meant for her. Her heart jumped painfully when a tall figure on horseback rode through the trees on the other side of the road; he did not see her, but she saw him. It was Richard Summerville and he seemed to be trying to lead the soldiers away from the group and after him instead.

But it was too late. Soon the soldiers appeared and she had no time to turn the cart or ride away before they were upon them. All Julia could do now was pray and that is what she did, prayed for a quick death. She could not know her prayers would be answered, and by an unexpected hand.

As they were led away to Caister Castle before being moved to London, Julia's thoughts were a jumble of memories of the joys and trials of her life. She had heard if the condemned recanted, declared themselves Catholic, they would be spared and she knew that is what Charles would have her do. She was unsure about that. Bethany would do it without hesitation, just as she had given up everything she held dear for the wealth on offer, but what about Julia? Did she want to be a martyr? Could she face the flames? She shivered with fear, told herself God knew what was in her heart.

Cranmer had recanted when his courage failed him, but it had not saved him. Mary had not believed him, but would she believe a farmer's wife, a woman too young to know her own mind? As it turned out, she was not given the choice.

Julia was taken to a small room where she was questioned for hours by a bishop who was not concerned whether she chose to recant; all he wanted to know was how to find Charles Carlisle.

So she had no choice, after all. She was not to be given the option of recanting, not unless she gave up the man she loved and all their friends with him. She would not do it, could not do it. She had heard of people dying of fright and wondered if she might be fortunate enough for the fear to stop her heart. She felt terrified enough for that; she had never been so afraid in her entire life.

She was given no food or drink and not allowed to relieve herself. She tried to hold on, but the warm flow soon soaked her skirt and made her feel even more miserable.

"Tell us where he is, Mistress, and you will be given refreshments and you will go free."

"I do not know him," she replied feebly. "I have told you and told you. I was on the road, alone and on foot, looking for a place to sleep for the night when the cart came. They were but giving me a ride, nothing more. I do not know this man of whom you speak."

She could see the Bishop's fat little fingers clenching into a fist, his ruby rings sparkling in the candlelight. Candlelight? Had she been here that long? She was dizzy and faint and could feel the chill of cold urine beneath her.

"You expect me to believe that a woman such as yourself was living out, a street dweller? Your hair is clean, your body is clean, even your teeth are white. You are lying and not very well."

She wondered why this so-called holy man did not use physical force, but perhaps this was worse. She would never tell him where Charles was, no matter what he did to her.

Her thoughts went to Anne Askew, a Protestant preacher who gave her life to satisfy King Henry's persecution, who bore the dubious distinction of being the only woman ever to be tortured on the rack. They had to carry her to the stake because they had dislocated all her limbs in their efforts to make her condemn Queen Catherine Parr as a heretic.

Mistress Askew was a martyr to their cause and would have been a saint had she been Catholic. The Pope believed he had the power to make saints, to elevate mortals to a special status in paradise; the Protestants had no such arrogance. They could only revere Anne's memory and remember her courage. If she could resist them, so could Julia. What she had so far suffered was comfort compared to that.

"Very well," the Bishop said. "I am going to have my dinner. Perhaps hunger and thirst will loosen your tongue by the time I return."

She was hungry and thirsty, but more than that she was more tired than she had ever been in her life before. She was relieved as she watched him go, then laid her head on her arms on the table and closed her eyes; but she was not to be allowed to sleep. One of the guards slammed his hand onto the table beside her head to wake her, then he left the room, muttering something to the other guard as he went. Probably going to the privy; he would not have to sit in his own urine while it grew cold and chilled his body.

She laid her head back down and tried to pray, but the words would not come. They were chased from her mind by thoughts of the horrifying death which awaited her, when she would be tied to a wooden stake and flames would rip through her skirts and sear her flesh. Her only hope was that the smoke might fill her lungs and choke her before she suffered too much, or that some kind soul might hang a bag of gunpowder around her waist to hasten her end.

There was no hope of rescue; had she been able, she might have recanted to save her life, for the sake of the people who loved her, for Charles and her little son. But they knew who she was; they knew she had been driving the cart and they had been expecting Charles, so it was obvious she was one of the leaders too.

Tears flooded from her eyes and onto her hand, but she made no move to wipe them away. That was when she felt someone beside her, felt a hand beside her ear and opened her eyes to see that hand putting a little clay bottle on the table.

She looked up to see the other guard smiling gently.

"It will not save you," he whispered. "But it may make things easier."

"What is it?"

"Smells like poppy juice, enough to numb the senses at least. Likely enough to finish you off if you are so inclined. You are advised to drink it all, but not too soon."

"Thank you."

"No need to thank me; I was well paid to take the risk."

She frowned, puzzled about who would do such a thing. Someone who could not help but wanted to, someone with enough money to be able to persuade this simple guard to risk his own safety to ease her way out of the world.

She recalled the night it had all gone wrong, the night she was arrested and the tall figure whose horse raced through the trees in a vain attempt to draw attention away from them, perhaps cause the soldiers to leave them and follow him. She recalled the familiar deep voice telling them to go back, but it was too late.

The last time she had heard that voice it was swearing fidelity and devotion to her sister in the small village church near her father's country house. A wave of gratitude washed over her as she tucked the vessel into her sleeve and laid her head down again, fell asleep wondering how she could take the potion without being seen.

***

It was a rough journey back to London and Julia had been given some sort of porridge and some dirty water before being thrust into the waiting coach with others. The soldiers did not want her to die of thirst before they got her to Smithfield. She was wet, cold and uncomfortable and sure she must stink of urine, but these good people had worse things to concern them.

They had left Caister after dark and most of them were exhausted, but there was no way to sleep on the hard bench and rickety, swaying vehicle. There were narrow, horizontal slits in the sides of the coach, up high near the ceiling, which would be the only source of light were it not pitch black outside.

It was silent in the coach, nobody spoke. There was nothing to say really, nothing at all. Many of them prayed, but Julia only closed her eyes and held tight to the bottle concealed within her sleeve.

As the vehicle drew to a stop, she was able to stand and see through the narrow slits that they had come straight here, to Smithfield, that the faggots were already being laid and as her friends stepped down one by one, their arms were grabbed by rough guards and pulled back, their wrists tied tightly behind their backs.

This was her chance, her only chance to drink the potent drug her former lover had smuggled into the castle for her. For the first time she wondered why. Was it for his wife's sake? Was it for the sake of that one afternoon they had spent in his bed, when he showed her what it felt like to be desired and wanted by a handsome and virile man?

Whatever it was, he had risked a great deal to do it. His face was well known, he could be easily recognised and the guard would have had to be very well paid to keep quiet. It was a small mercy, but Julia was grateful for it.

She turned away from the doorway and pulled the clay bottle from her sleeve, pulled the cork and tilted back her head to drink the contents. It was a nasty, bitter taste, but she began to feel the effects straight away. She would have to be carried if they did not get on with it, as the drug was already taking hold.

The prisoners were all loaded into an open cart, much like the one she had been driving when the soldiers caught them, only in this one they all had to stand. Everything was beginning to blur and Julia was not sure how long she could stand, especially with the rocking from side to side as the horse pulled them over the rough road.

She could smell burning flesh, a sick, sweet smell, she could hear screams and she could see hundreds of people and hear their cheers. What were they cheering for? Did they not realise they could be next? It would not take much for the Fanatic to turn on all her subjects.

Then she heard her name being called. She took no notice at first, thinking this drug she had been given must have some sort of hallucinatory powers. But it came again, as clear as the screams from the condemned: 'Julia!'

The voice was familiar and closer now; Julia turned, looked down to see a woman, a beautiful woman with dark hair and dressed in beautiful clothes, her gloved hands clutching the side of the rough wooden cart. That was good, Julia thought. Good that she wore gloves or she could splinter her hands on that wood.

She wondered what someone so obviously wealthy was doing there, holding fast to the cart, amid all those sweaty bodies. She was beautifully dressed; dressed like a countess. She shook her head to clear it a little and her eyes grew wide. A countess? It was Bethany; it was her own dear sister. She recalled their last meeting, the last words she had spoken to her were harsh, unfair, but she had meant them at the time.

Then she heard a man's voice, saw him grip Bethany's arm and pull her away.

"My Lady!" He called. "Come away! You do not want to join her, do you?"

Julia tried to smile, to reassure her, but she did not think she had managed it. Her face was too numb now, her whole body felt that it was fading away from existence and she would soon evaporate.

She was pulled roughly from the cart and dragged to the piled faggots. The guard likely thought she was resisting; he had no way of knowing she was half asleep and that when he tied her hands to the wooden stake, she was unconscious before he walked away.

CHAPTER NINE

Charles heard the whispering from his bed at the top of the stairs. He listened carefully; although they tried to keep their voices low, his friends' words were clear. She was gone. His beloved Julia, the love of his life, his beautiful lady who never knew a moment's thought for her own importance, who had given him everything and he had let her go.

He should have stopped her, should have done something. It was true she was the only one educated enough to get passed the guards, but it had not worked, had it? They had all died and now he was left with her little son, with the awful and thankless task of telling him his mother was not coming back.

From the moment she had ridden into his yard, back there in his father's farm, he had been afraid of losing her, but he never expected to lose her like this. How she must have suffered! Simon would not know about her suffering, not until he was a grown man and old enough to hear it.

Tears filled his eyes; he did not even have a portrait of her. He had nothing but his memories of these short, blissful years which would never come again.

On the small cupboard in the corner of the room was her hairbrush. He picked it up and ran a finger over the long, pale blonde strands caught up in the bristles, all he had left of her. He took the brush and locked it away in the chest with her clothes.

His shoulder was still stiff and painful, and he likely needed to give it more time to heal, but anger was rapidly mixing with his grief and he wanted to hurt something or someone. In his mind, there was but one person who was responsible for this, one person who would be made to pay no matter what the cost or risk to himself.

He struggled down the narrow staircase and went outside where Emily leapt forward to help him.

"You should not be out of bed," she scolded.

"Should I stay here and let the Arch Papist get away my wife's murder?"

"You heard."

"Look after Simon, please," he said as he made his way to the stables.

"Where are you going?" Emily called after him. "You cannot tackle the Earl all alone; he is a warrior, a skilled soldier. You will be killed; is that what she would have wanted?"

He ignored her, did not even glance back as he continued towards the stables. He led out Guinevere. She was a little small for him, but the only one in the stables schooled to be ridden.

"You are not going alone," a man's voice called after him.

Then there was a small crowd, two of the men hitching the cart to the Shire horse while he tacked up Julia's little mare.

"I will care for you, girl," he whispered to the animal. "You have no need to worry."

She had loved this mare; he would teach Simon how to ride her. That would be a good tribute to her and it would give him something to do to take the child's mind off his loss. Simon was very young still and would soon forget her, but Charles could help him do that by caring for her mare.

The party arrived at Summerville Hall after an easy enough journey. They were but a few miles away and Charles only wondered now how Sir Geoffrey had failed to find them again. Perhaps he had given up looking, although it seemed unlikely. He was determined to not only find Julia, but to punish her harshly as well. Charles would not have let that happen; there was no way he was going to carry out his threat. Charles would kill him first.

Julia had told him about the private church built in the woods, in among the trees and he rode straight there. He glanced at the small cottage beside it, just to be sure no one was there. The heavy oak doors to the church were standing open; Summerville had no reason to lock them, had he?

They had already smashed several statues and overturned the altar before they noticed Father O'Neil, praying before a statue of the Virgin Mary in the far corner. He was on his knees and he turned, his eyes wide and fearful.

Charles held up a hand to stop his followers from approaching. The little priest looked terrified and he wanted to assure him that he meant him no harm. It was not the priest's fault his beloved Julia was dead, was it?

He took one step toward him, his hand out to help him to his feet but he got no closer before the priest clutched at his chest and keeled over onto the hard stone floor.

***

Charles held fast to his grief for Simon's sake, tried his best to conceal his feelings from the boy. Each time he looked at the child he was reminded of his enemy; it was intolerable and he could only hope he would change as time went by. Perhaps his hair would lighten to match his mother's, perhaps his features would grow more like hers; it had been known for a child's whole face to change in these formative years. But distressing though his looks were, they did not stop Charles from loving him. He was a delightful child and Julia had loved him; Charles would continue to love him, no matter what.

He looked from the window to be sure Simon was safely being cared for by Emily and he saw the horse approaching, a single horse with a single rider. Lady Summerville! He watched her as she peered into the open doors of the small cottages, watched as she turned suddenly and saw the smoke coming from the manor house chimney.

His anger rose. How dare she come here? How dare she come to remind him of his loss, to remind him of what her husband had done. Julia told him why Bethany married the Earl and he watched her approach with contempt in his heart. Julia also told him that she believed her sister loved the man. That alone was enough to make him despise her; how could she love a man who would do the things he had done? How could any woman love such a man?

A sudden fear touched his heart. If she knew Julia was dead, had she come for her son? She was not taking Simon! He was all he had left of the woman he loved and he would never let him go. Perhaps Summerville knew of his existence, perhaps he had sent her to bring him back to him.

He stepped outside, glanced across the fields to where Simon was trying to help the men mend the fences and knew the little boy was safe for now. He leaned against the door frame with his arms folded until Julia's sister drew rein beside him.

"What brings you here, My Lady?" He asked angrily as she approached. "Your husband has done untold damage to my family. Does he now send you to finish us off?"

"No!" She cried, shaking her head.

"Julia is dead. She told me what you did for Summerville's wealth and title; I hope you are content with your dirty bargain."

"I know she is dead, Sir," she answered bitterly. "I watched her die."

His expression softened suddenly and he took one step toward her, then he offered his hand to help her down.

"You can dismount, My Lady," he said quietly. "I will not harm you if indeed you speak the truth."

She got down hesitantly.

"I promise you, Mr Carlisle," she said swiftly, "I have not seen His Lordship in many months. I came to enquire about the child, to be sure he is safe for Julia's sake. That is all."

He relaxed a little but wanted to be clear that she was taking Simon nowhere.

"I will care for him, you may be sure of that. It is what she would have wanted. He is safe with me, so long as his father never learns of his existence."

She looked doubtful, and it seemed to him she was trying to decide how much to reveal.

"I know he is Lord Summerville's son," he said, "if that is what you are concerned about."

"You know?"

"Of course. I am not blind, but his parentage is hardly the child's fault and I love him as I would love my own. I will not blame the child for his birth, you can be sure of that." He watched her for a few minutes, wondering if she had more to say, then an irony occurred to him and he smiled. "I think it rather divine justice that the only son of the Arch Papist should be raised as a Protestant."

She caught her breath and he could tell his words had sparked her anger. So, she still loved the Earl, even after everything.

"I hope you have purer reasons for raising the boy than to avenge yourself on Richard," she said angrily.

He gave a small, self-derisive laugh.

"You have every right, I suppose, to suspect me of that. But rest assured, that is not my motive. It is merely a bonus."

She looked alarmed for a moment and Charles expected her to mount her mare and ride away, but instead she drew a deep breath as if to give herself courage.

"Tell me one thing, Sir," she began. "What had Julia done to become so prominent? You are here, you have survived. What did she do to draw attention to herself?"

Yes, he had survived, he who should have been the one to be arrested and executed. But he had allowed her to go instead and now he had to tell her sister he had been too damned weak to protect her.

"She was discovered helping a group of Protestants to flee to the coast," he said at last. "I should have been the one to go, but I was wounded. She insisted on going in my place and I have to live with that guilt for the rest of my life."

Bethany felt the tears brimming and glanced away to hide them.

"And it was you and your people who vandalised the church at Summerville, in retaliation?"

He nodded.

"Petty, was it not?" He said. "It was a personal revenge and not one I had any right to involve my people in. I am sorry about the priest though. He seemed a harmless little man."

Bethany seemed to be deep in thought for a few moments, her beautiful face marred by a frown of concentration. When at last she spoke, Charles was shocked but intrigued.

"The church will not be repaired," she said quickly. "Not yet anyway. There is a little cottage in the forest just next to it and there is an underground passage from the house to the crypt." Charles stood frowning at her. "Can we not do something with that?" She went on. "Can we not use it to help more Protestants out of England?"

He studied her for a few moment, suspecting a trap, but if anything she looked uncertain, even distressed. Despite the vast difference in their looks and colouring, she reminded him of Julia; perhaps it was because they had been raised from birth together, but her obvious sadness made him want to gather her into his arms and comfort her.

Ridiculous idea. He was but a farmer, she a countess dressed in brocade and velvet.

"Why would you do this?" He asked. "Julia told me you loved your husband; she said you were very much in love with him. Has that changed?"

"No. I cannot tell how Julia knew that, but she was right."

"Then why?"

"I want to do this for Julia; it has nothing to do with Richard or my love for him. I will love him until the end of my days and I would gladly die for him, but alas he does not feel the same. He does not love me in return, but it is not for revenge that I make this offer."

"What then?"

"I want to help. I think my plan will work and we will be able to help more Protestants to safety. Is that not worth the risk?"

***

Charles sent a man to help her, a working class man called Martin who hated Catholics and was suspicious of Bethany, of the Countess who would go against her husband's wishes to help his enemies.

The scheme worked well and many hundreds of Protestants were helped out of England by the scheme, while Charles had his own base some few miles away and they doubled the amount of people they helped to safety.

But the day came when a parchment scroll was shot into the front door of the manor house with an arrow. It was a clear warning to stay away from Summerville Hall and the cottage in the woods, to leave the church alone and send no more refugees that way.

She had been discovered, that was obvious and Charles felt very guilty for ever involving her, even though it was her own idea. He had caused her sister's death and now likely hers. What would her husband do with her? How would he punish her for her treachery? He had no doubt the Earl would think of some barbaric punishment to inflict on his wife; he might even have her arrested and allow her to suffer the flames like her sister.

He remembered Sir Geoffrey Winterton sitting atop his horse in Charles' yard, informing him in detail what he intended for Julia. Would Richard Summerville do something similar? But it was not adultery of which Bethany was guilty, and it was not theft either. It was treason and heresy, punishable by death, a horrible, painful death.

She told him the Earl did not return her love, but would he condemn her to the same fate as her sister? Was he that barbaric? Or would he feel the shame of his wife's crime becoming public knowledge?

Charles' glance fell on Simon where he practiced brushing Guinevere's legs as Charles had taught him. The sight of the boy filled Charles with fury; Lord Summerville was to blame for all this! He had married one sister, tried to bend her to his papist will, fathered a child on the other sister and sent her to the stake. Just what more did the man want from them? And how could Bethany really love such a monster?

He decided it was safest to postpone all evacuation plans until he knew what was happening. It was possible Bethany would be forced to give up the location of Sinclair Manor; it was possible she would be tortured for the information. He shuddered; if she were in danger of that, Julia would also have been in danger of it. He could not bear the idea; he had to believe she did not suffer that as well or he might just lose what little sanity he still retained.

It was a few weeks after, with no word to set his mind at ease, that Charles sent a friend disguised as a pedlar, to try to discover the whereabouts of Lady Summerville. He was to call at the house, at the servants' entrance and discreetly begin a conversation which might lead him to the truth.

Charles almost fainted with relief when his friend returned with the news that Her Ladyship was living at court with His Lordship.

So, she was safe and they had reconciled. He could not understand how that had happened, but perhaps she had been wrong; perhaps he did love her in return.

Charles resumed evacuations, but he needed to be able to help more people to safety. As the year wore on, he thought often of the little cottage, the church and wondered if he could perhaps find a use for them. Lord Summerville was in London, as was his wife; if he was careful he might manage to go undetected.

So he set out to investigate the possibility. He tied Guinevere to a branch and crept forward to the small hovel. He wanted to do his best for the little mare, but he knew she was too small for him. Still, riding her made him feel closer to Julia somehow, and it would not be long before Simon would be big enough to ride her himself.

He was approaching the cottage, looking down to avoid treading on any twigs and making a noise, when he saw smoke rising from the makeshift chimney, a hole in the thatched roof. Someone was living there. He stood and watched as a figure approached from the direction of the church, a woman with a basket in her arms, a basket filled with vegetables which she took inside the cottage.

Charles could scarcely believe his eyes; it was Bethany. He stayed where he was for a long time, seated on the damp grass and hidden behind the trees. He saw her come out of the cottage again and make her way to the church with her basket; this time she returned with logs, and she held the handle of the basket over one arm while her other hand supported the bottom. Obviously, it was heavy, perhaps too heavy for her.

His mind was full of possible reasons why the Countess of Summerville was dressed as a peasant and carrying raw vegetables and heavy logs into a hovel barely fit for habitation. So she was not living at Whitehall after all, so she had not reconciled with her husband. Charles suspected the Earl had imprisoned his wife here and his anger swelled. He had been wrong, the man did not love her.

Or perhaps she had escaped his wrath and taken refuge here, hidden herself away disguised as a peasant in the hope that he did not find her.

She came out again after a while and disappeared into the trees on the other side of the little building. When she did not come back, he got to his feet and went to investigate. Inside the fire was barely cold, the food basket rested on the bed in the corner. He opened the wooden chest at the bottom of the bed and saw among the peasant's garb a blue velvet gown, with pearl trimming.

He had no wish to frighten her if she returned and found someone here, so he went outside and waited behind the wall for her return. At last he peered around the corner and saw her walking slowly towards him, a wistful little smile on her lovely face.

He called out softly.

"Charles? What are you doing here?"

She took his hand and pulled him inside, looking about anxiously.

"I have been watching this place," he told her, "hoping to find a way to use it again. Imagine my surprise to find you here."

"No," she replied shaking her head. "No way in the world can this place ever be used again. It would be the death of us both." She paused and looked up at him. "How are you still alive? Richard discovered me, discovered our plan. I never knew what happened to the poor souls who were waiting for the next trip out, or what happened to Martin. I suppose they are all dead."

He wore a little puzzled frown as he shook his head.

"We had word, a warning to cancel that night's evacuation and all future ones. I assumed it came from you. I knew the Earl had discovered what we were doing, I was told. I worried about what had happened to you, but when I enquired, I had word you were living with him at court."

She laughed derisively, giving the impression he had been mistaken.

"I have been watching you for hours," he went on, "gathering kindling, carrying logs and food from the church door like any peasant. I could not believe it was you." His eyes swept her clothing, then looked around the cottage with a grimace. "Are you hiding, or has he imprisoned you here to live like this?" He said with a frown of disgust. "His own wife?"

"Do not fret, Charles. It is better than the alternative."

He raised his eyebrows in surprise. Her words could mean only one thing; her husband had threatened her life and judging by her demeanour, she did not doubt him.

"You fear for your safety?" He asked with a frown of concern. "Then do not stay. Come with me; you can help more with the cause."

She shook her head vigorously, looking suddenly terrified.

"No, Charles. I am not brave enough for that. I must stay here, live like this. It is my punishment for betraying him, but when I think what happened to my sister, I feel myself very fortunate."

"But you put yourself in danger every time you send me warnings. Do you not know that? If His Lordship would condemn his wife to the life of a peasant, he would surely have no hesitation in charging you with treason."

She stared at him for a few moments, a little puzzled frown on her brow.

"Of what warnings do you speak, Charles? I know nothing about this."

"What?" He looked startled. "I have been receiving them for months now, letters usually left at the door during the night. Sometimes they have been shot with an arrow into the doorframe."

She laughed.

"I have never been proficient in archery. What sort of warnings?"

"Warnings that have saved the lives of our people. Little notes that give details of when the Queen's men are going to be in certain places, when they could have caught us all. Sometimes they have forestalled a planned trip, sometimes they are of no use whatsoever." He turned away briefly, then looked back at her. "If not you, then who?"

"I have no idea, Charles. Be sure that I have not been privy to the sort of knowledge you speak of. I have not left this place for almost a year. The Queen could be dead for all I know."

"Sadly, no," he replied, shaking his head. "I was sure it was you. Who on earth else would be doing this?"

She shrugged.

"I have no idea. I do not know who would have the knowledge but secretly be on our side."

He wanted desperately to help her. He looked about at the poor dwelling, looked at her drab clothing, at her pale complexion, and he could not bear the thought of leaving her here to suffer like this. He was but a poor farmer, but even his field hands lived better than this. He had to do something! He had to try.

"So will you let me take you away from this place?" Charles asked quietly.

"No," she replied. "My little girl is here. I will not leave her."

A child? Why had he never known about a child? Because he had never asked, that was why.

"Forgive me," he said at last. "I did not know you had a child."

"Why should you? We know little about each other really, do we?"

"Then she is Simon's half-sister," he said quietly. "What a very strange idea."

On impulse, he pulled her toward him and held her close, not in any passionate way but as a brother might hold a much loved sister. He felt her press herself against him, felt her need to draw more comfort from him and he was happy to give it. After a few minutes, she drew away from him.

"I shall take my leave then," he murmured. "I see I am putting you in danger by simply being here. But I still have no idea who our friend at court might be."

She watched as he crept through the trees, her expression wistful and sad and she had no idea she was being carefully and quietly observed.

***

Adrian Kennington stood watching the silent hovel for a few moments more before he made his way back to his horse. He had followed Charles Carlisle, as Lord Summerville had requested, and he had led him here, to Richard's own land, to Richard's own wife.

He was angry because they had more important things to do than follow a man who could well be Lady Summerville's lover and he was angry on her behalf when he saw the living conditions to which his friend had condemned her. A countess should not be living like this, no matter what harm she had done her husband.

He desperately wanted to help her, to do something to ease her lot, but what? He could hardly remove her from the place without Richard finding out and it was really none of his business. He had enough to concern him in his own marriage without worrying about his friend's and he could do nothing about either while this Queen still lived.

He had no way of knowing he would not have much longer to wait, that the end of this year would see the end of Mary and her inquisition.

CHAPTER TEN

News of the death of Queen Mary reached Sinclair Manor only a few hours after it happened. It was momentous news which spread throughout the country like a fire and when Charles heard, he smiled for the first time since Julia died. He picked up her little son and held him close, kissed his cheek, then set him gently down again. Simon was growing fast and was almost too big now for Charles to lift, and his colouring was slowly changing; his hair was no longer as dark as it had been, but he still resembled his natural father too much for Charles' liking.

He went inside the house and sat at the table. It was chilly and he would light the fire later, but for now he wanted to ponder this news and decide how best to proceed into the future. Nobody had come to claim this house in all the time they had been here, but now the reign was over that could change. He would have liked to be able to feel secure here, to feel settled, but that was not possible.

His father's farm was still his own. He could take Simon and anyone else who wanted to come and return there, but no doubt Julia's legal husband still had that warrant for his arrest. He did sell stolen jewellery belonging to him after all and he wondered if the man would still be interested in executing that warrant. He no longer had a claim on his wife, could no longer threaten Julia with his barbaric punishments. She had moved beyond the reach of any man, but it was still within his power to ease his frustration for that on Charles.

Charles decided he would stay for a little while, see what happened. If anyone did come along to claim back Sinclair Manor, he could think then of returning to the farm. For now, he had to put the past behind him and do his best to raise Julia's son to be the man she wanted him to be.

***

Adrian kissed Elizabeth gently and left her to finish dressing. She had sent for him after their long estrangement because his son was dangerously ill, but thank God the boy had recovered. Instead of the tragedy he has dreaded on his journey here, she had given him the greatest gift of all this day; she had allowed him a second chance and he would not fail her.

"Your mother will disapprove of you taking me to bed in the daylight," she said playfully.

He shrugged.

"It is none of her business. It was her meddling that came between us before; I'll not let her do it again."

Elizabeth was not going to argue about it, not now they were trying to rebuild their marriage, but had Adrian told her about Marianne, they might not have parted. It was hardly fair to blame the Dowager Lady Kennington for that.

Downstairs he was greeted by the angry scowl of his mother. The older she got, it seemed the more permanent that scowl and Adrian had not forgiven her for breaking into his desk and finding letters from his former mistress. That had driven the final wedge between himself and his beloved wife, and this reconciliation would not be spoiled by her or anyone else.

"So you have returned, then?" The Dowager asked. "Is it for good? Will you return to your marriage and at least spare me more disgrace."

He continued down the stairs and kissed his mother on the cheek.

"It is wonderful to see you, too, My Lady," he said.

"Do you realise what you have done? Allowing your wife to leave you when we were already the gossip of the neighbourhood."

He frowned. What on earth was the woman talking about?

"It is true, Adrian," Frances spoke from the sitting room doorway. "I am afraid people still disapprove of my living here."

Frances had been Adrian's betrothed until she fell in love with his brother and eloped with him to the New World. Society was not happy about

Adrian's agreement to allow her to live in his house when his brother died; neither was the Dowager Lady Kennington.

She told them all from the beginning that Frances would never be accepted, that her children would never find suitable marriage partners. Adrian had taken little notice; his mother was always very aware of her own importance, her own place in society and he believed she was only angry that he did not agree with her.

"After all this time?" He said incredulously.

"I told you what would happen!" The Dowager declared. "I told you when you let her move back here how it would be, but you refused to listen."

"And you have done nothing to fuel the fire, I suppose?" Adrian asked suspiciously.

"Me?" His mother said defensively. "Why would I?"

"Why not? It proved you right."

Old Lady Kennington glanced at Frances disapprovingly, her arm out as she gestured toward her.

"She does not even try to fit back in," she declared. "Look at the way she dresses! A lady should be dressed properly, like Elizabeth; Frances looks like a peasant."

Adrian noticed Frances' attire for the first time and saw that she was dressed in simple linens, a pretty gown but not the sort a lady of the nobility should wear.

"I think that is a little harsh, Mother," he protested. "And anyway, what difference do her clothes make? Perhaps she would dress up if she thought she had anything to dress up for."

"Please," Frances pulled on his sleeve. "Do not argue over me. Your mother is right; as far as anyone who matters is concerned, I am an adulteress for eloping with Mark. They refuse to recognise my marriage to him. Our own betrothal was not much different to a marriage, apparently."

"Unconsummated it was no marriage," Adrian said.

"Do you not see," Frances said. "In their eyes, you and I were wed. That makes what I did with Mark not only adultery but incest too. I am shunned."

He put his arm around her shoulders and hugged her, a gesture she felt surprisingly comforting. She had tried to stand alone since she lost Mark, tried to be independent and needing of no one, but this small comfort suddenly meant the world to her.

"You do not want to be bothered with my troubles when you have only just arrived home." She smiled and reached up to kiss his cheek. "I am so pleased for you both."

"I am the luckiest man alive," he said. "My dear Elizabeth believes me worthy of another chance; I will not fail her a second time. Perhaps now I am back, we can begin to look to a real future, I can do something about your situation."

"It is of no matter to me, Adrian," she said. "But the children are growing fast. What sort of life will they have?"

Old Lady Kennington scoffed loudly and walked with the aid of her stick towards the back of the house. Adrian had not noticed that before; she now needed a walking stick.

When Mark died in the New World, Frances had no other thought but to return to England with his children, to beg his brother for help in his memory. Adrian had been more than kind, but he had no idea how she felt. She felt a burden; old Lady Kennington was right to suppose she would be shunned and Frances' presence in the house put her in a precarious position of her own.

Frances wanted to do something to ease the burden, but she had nothing and even if she had, she felt out of place in noble circles now. She and Mark had built a farm together, had lived as farmers with no affectations of position and they had been happy. Here she felt herself in a foreign land with no knowledge of the language.

She was doing Elizabeth no favours either. People thought it very odd that she should welcome her husband's former betrothed and it cast doubt on the legality of her own marriage. It was wrong that their lives and happiness, their acceptance should depend on the opinions of others. That is what she missed about her life with Mark, as well as the man himself; there nobody cared who you were or whether you belonged.

They went into the sitting room and sat before the fire, watched the children playing in the gardens outside the window.

"I wrote to my father," Frances said. "I told him he had grandchildren. I even begged his forgiveness for all the trouble I caused and you know what he said?" Adrian shook his head but he could easily guess. "He wrote back that I must have made a mistake, that he had no daughter. I have tried, Adrian, but if you are going to be here, it is going to be worse for both of us, me and Elizabeth."

"I suppose they must think of her as living in sin as well," Adrian remarked with a sardonic smile.

"They may well do, but they respect her. They have no respect at all for me or for my children."

The voice from the bottom of the stairs stopped him from saying the same thing.

"We will work something out for you, Frances," Elizabeth said. "Now Adrian is home, we can see what can be done. Would you consider a new marriage?"

Frances smiled then shook her head.

"No one of your acquaintance will want me, that is for certain," she said. "And after the years on the farm, I am not sure I would fit into that life any more."

Adrian took her hand and squeezed it reassuringly. He could hardly believe that after all this time people would not accept Frances back into society.

But her feeling of being in limbo, without a place and with nowhere to go, was soon to change to one of hope.

The following day, Elizabeth received a letter from a London lawyer, telling her that Elliot had been missing for seven years, the time the law allowed before someone could be presumed dead. That being the case, as his lawyer he had opened Elliot's Will and wrote to ask for a meeting.

"What do you suppose it means?" She asked Adrian.

"Well, since the traitor wiped out his entire family and has no one else, I imagine you are his main beneficiary."

"I do not want anything from him!" She cried.

"Nevertheless, if he has named you in his Will, you should see what he has left. You can do some charity work with it if nothing else. Think how many Protestants have lost their possessions during the Papist reign. That would be a fitting tribute to the Sinclair family."

Elizabeth smiled at the idea, then kissed Adrian's cheek affectionately. She wanted to kiss him properly; having him back meant the world to her and she only wished she had listened to him when he told her about his mistress. He had sworn it was but one indiscretion, one temptation when things between him and his wife were strained, but she had not believed him. She was too hurt, her trust had been betrayed again and she could not forgive that.

They went to London to meet with Elliot's lawyer. The journey was not a long one, but as they approached the city, Adrian was half surprised to see no smoke on the horizon, no stench of burning flesh. He shivered. He had always loved the capital city, but now it was spoilt in his memory and he hoped never to see it again.

The carriage reached the address on the letter before Adrian realised it was but a few streets away from the rooms he had kept for Marianne, his mistress. He glanced hesitantly at Elizabeth, hoping she did not connect this place with that terrible afternoon when she had caught him in the act of betraying her. He put his arm around her and hugged her close, relieved that she did not seem to notice where she was.

The lawyer's office was up a narrow staircase in one of those black and white buildings with the upper floors hanging over the street, just like the rooms where he had kept his mistress, just like that same room where he had lost his Elizabeth because he could not keep his hands off Marianne.

He hoped this meeting would not take long.

"My Lady, My Lord," the lawyer greeted them and gestured to a settle along the wall beside his desk. "Lord Elliot's Will is simple enough and will not take long to explain. He has left everything he has to you, My Lady, with a message. It is a simple message; it says only: *forgive me.* I imagine we all know what that means."

"I know what he meant by it, yes," Elizabeth replied. "But I cannot comply. What precisely has he left and what happens now?"

"The first thing to do is to have him legally declared dead. Once that is done, I can arrange to have ownership of Sinclair Manor transferred to you."

"Sinclair Manor?" Adrian said with a frown.

Elizabeth turned to look at him with a nod.

"His father's manor house, from where they were taken," she said. "Is something wrong?"

"No, nothing."

But he recognised the name at once and hoped it was another house and estate called Sinclair Manor, for that was the name of the house from whence he had followed the Protestant leader, Charles Carlisle. The house would not be empty, as Elizabeth supposed, and since Carlisle had been living there, what was the likelihood that he had killed Elliot in order to take over the house?

Adrian waited until they were home again, all the children in bed, supper eaten and he had retreated to his bedchamber with his wife. He still found it hard to believe that he was finally here, after the years of separation, and he wanted nothing to spoil that.

They had made love as they had when they were first wed, with all the passion and desire two people in love could have for each other and the feel of her flesh next to his, of her lips on his chest, was paradise on earth.

They both lie beneath the covers, his arm around her, her head resting on his broad chest. He would have to tell her but he wanted to leave the past buried where it belonged; unfortunately that was not an option.

"What are you going to do with the house?" He asked.

"I have been thinking about that," she answered. "I thought we might let Frances have it."

He sat up and looked down at her with a frown. He had not expected that, not at all, but it was a wonderful idea.

"She could live there with the children," Elizabeth went on. "She could call herself the widow she is and there would be no one to criticise. She would need help; it is farmland after all, but at least no one would be calling her an adulteress and accusing her of incest. What do you think?"

"I think it is wonderful of you and very generous, but…"

"But?"

So he told her about Charles Carlisle, about how Richard Summerville had asked him to follow him, about how he had followed him from Sinclair Manor. He did not tell her where he had followed him to, as it did not seem appropriate; it was Richard's secret, not his. But then, it was keeping secrets that had led to their rift before and he vowed never to do that again.

He decided to tell her everything, how he thought the man was Lady Summerville's lover, how he had followed him to her prison in the woods. She caught her breath, reached up to stroke his shoulder.

"It is all right," he told her. "She was back where she belongs when the Queen died and he was back with her. We can only wish them well."

"If she can forgive such treatment, she must love him as much as I love you," she said softly.

He kissed her, slipped his hand beneath the covers to caress her breast.

"I will go alone," he said. "To Sinclair Manor. It could be dangerous."

"No. I will come and bring Frances with me, if it is what she wants. If this man is still there, we will discuss things, perhaps see if he can be persuaded to leave."

***

Charles had just finished breakfast when he heard the horses and carriage draw up. His heart leapt and he quickly ran to the window to be sure Simon was out in the fields with some of the men, not here in the house where he could be claimed by Sir Geoffrey Winterton. He lived in fear that the man would find him, destroy his quiet life by serving his warrant.

He saw at once it was not Winterton and he relaxed a little. Still the carriage was of superior make and the man who rode before it had the dress and bearing of the nobility. He stood in the courtyard and frowned at the approaching party, his arms folded.

"I am Adrian," the man said as he dismounted, "Earl of Kennington." Charles nodded. "And you are Charles Carlisle."

Charles frowned suspiciously before replying. "I am, My Lord. What can I do for you?"

"It is complicated. May we come inside?"

Charles looked passed him to where a lady with blonde waves in her shiny hair stepped down from the carriage. She was dressed in red velvet and she greeted him with a warm smile which put his mind at ease.

As she put her feet firmly on the ground, she turned back to the carriage and another woman followed her down the step. This one looked a little less elegant, her gown of printed linen, more of the farmer class but wealthier. Still her smile was warm and he could not help but wonder what her position was with this noble couple. She too was blonde, but neither of these women had hair like his Julia.

He shook his head to clear it of her memory. Whatever these people wanted, he could not afford to break down before them.

He poured wine, likely not the sort they were accustomed to but the best he could manage and they all sat at the table and eyed each other suspiciously.

"I will come straight to the point, Sir," Adrian said. "I know what an important part you played in the recent reign; I know you are responsible for the survival of hundreds, if not thousands of Protestants and we all owe you a debt which can never be repaid."

Charles neither expected nor wanted thanks; he had paid dearly for his role in the resistance and he needed no praise from anyone. He had done what needed to be done, as had Julia.

"You are Protestant then?" Charles asked quickly.

"We are."

"And have you come here simply to thank me?" Charles asked. "Or have you another motive?"

"The fact is, Elliot Sinclair, who owned this house, has been declared dead and has left his entire estate to my wife, to whom he was once betrothed."

Charles drew a quick breath then sipped his wine before he gazed compassionately at Elizabeth.

"My neighbour, Jacob told me what happened," he said. "I did wonder if anyone would turn up to claim the place. I did not kill your betrothed, My Lady. I did find him hanging from the rafters though."

Elizabeth gasped and Frances caught her hand.

"He killed himself?" She said.

Frances soft voice seemed to draw Charles' attention and his heart skipped. Her lovely, round face beneath her blonde curls made him smile; she was the first woman he had taken notice of since Julia and now he could not take his eyes off her.

"Mr Carlisle," Adrian said. "We can see how much work you have done here and we have no wish to evict you, but.."

"But nothing," Elizabeth interrupted. She turned to Frances, who nodded. "You have done heroic things for the Protestants and you have kept this place as best you can. If you wish to stay, we will not hinder you."

Elizabeth looked around the vast hall, her eyes moved to the stairs and the rafter beside it. That must be where Elliot's body hung rotting, until this man had come and found him. Up those stairs was her bedchamber, the chamber she had slept in from the time she first came to live here.

She had a vague memory of Elliot sneaking into that chamber one night, one of the last nights before he decided to commit the ultimate betrayal. He had wanted to share her bed, before the marriage, tried to convince her it was what everybody did. She refused, but she should have known then he was not to be trusted. Instead, in her vanity, she had simply believed he loved her too much to wait.

She dragged her attention back to the present company.

Charles bowed his head as he spoke.

"That is kind, My Lady, but it is your house. I can return to my father's farm if necessary. My son and I will be happy enough there."

"You have a son?" Frances asked.

This young woman intrigued Charles. He had still not guessed at her true role in the family; he had thought at first she was a servant, but she showed no servile deference and spoke her thoughts without fear of rebuke.

He looked passed her to the doorway where Simon stood watching and he held out his hand to the boy in greeting.

"My son, Simon," he announced and the child ran forward and climbed onto his lap.

Adrian recognised him at once but made no remark on it. This was Richard Summerville's son, there was no doubt about that. This was why it was so important to keep Charles Carlisle alive and free; it had nothing to do with the Protestant cause.

Now he was more mystified than ever. His mind was busy trying to work out where everyone fitted in this scenario; he had thought Carlisle to be Lady Summerville's lover, but now he found the man was raising the son of her husband. But who was the boy's mother?

He was trying to think of a civil way to learn the answer, but Frances was not prepared to wait.

"Where is his mother?" She asked boldly.

She no longer adhered to the niceties of the aristocracy; in the New World if you wanted to know something you asked. Since she had not been accepted back into that aristocratic world, she saw no reason to change that now.

"Dead," Charles replied.

"Forgive me," she said, but she did not drop her gaze as would be expected after such a remark. She kept her eyes on Charles Carlisle, on his handsome face, his luxuriant dark auburn hair and beard and he smiled with amusement.

"She was a martyr," he said, then glanced quickly at little Simon, wishing he had not said that in front of the boy.

Frances eyes filled with quick tears of compassion for the loss of this child's mother. The thought which leapt into her mind was voiced before she had time to stop and think about it. She had been searching for a place for herself and her children since the day she returned to England and now it seemed she was being presented with just such a place. She was not about to let it pass her by for the sake of false civility.

She could do a lot worse. She had enjoyed the farm in the Americas, so that would be no hardship and this man was very attractive. So far he had also seemed to be a kind man, a man who loved his son and the child appeared happy and healthy. Yes, he would make a good father for Mark's children.

"My children have no father," she said impulsively. "Yours has no mother. I think we could help each other."

Adrian stared at Frances in disbelief. His glance moved from her to Charles, to Elizabeth and back again, searching their expressions for a hint of their thoughts.

Charles smiled slightly, as though finding the suggestion amusing; Elizabeth looked as shocked as Adrian but Frances was smiling at their host, a little enigmatic smile which told Adrian she knew exactly what she was doing.

"Frances, Mr Carlisle does not understand your sense of humour as we do," Adrian said. "Perhaps we should talk in private."

"I will go," Charles said. "Give you some privacy."

They watched him in silence as he left the house, his smile growing as he went, then turned back to Frances.

"What are you doing?" Adrian demanded.

"Finding myself a suitable husband," she answered mischievously. "He is in need of a wife and a mother for his child. I am in need of a husband and a father for mine. What could be better?"

"Do you not think you should learn something about him first?"

"Why? I knew nothing about you when I was told I was to marry you."

"Yes and look how that turned out."

"Adrian," she said, putting her hand over his. "He is a hero, you said so yourself. I will never get over Mark and judging by the look in his eyes when I asked about Simon's mother, he will never get over her either."

"You put the man in a very difficult position," Elizabeth said. "I do think you should give him a fair opportunity to refuse."

"Besides," Adrian said with a shamefaced look. "You are of the nobility, or have you forgotten that? He is a farmer."

"So was Mark," Frances retorted. "And I am a farmer's widow. I no longer fit into your world, Adrian, and your world do not want me. I am a pariah, an outcast and while that suits me, I have to think of my children, of Mark's children. They have no place; this is my chance to give them one."

***

Charles was still smiling when he left his strange visitors to talk, taking Simon with him. If Lady Elizabeth wanted the house back, there was nothing he could do about it and he still had his father's farm, though lord knows what sort of state it would be in. He also feared Julia's husband might still look for him there, but it was a chance he would have to take.

But the woman they brought with them was intriguing. Her clothing was not of the elegant fabrics that Lady Elizabeth wore, although it was neat and clean enough, much as the women here wore, as Julia had worn towards the end, and Charles had believed her to be a servant. But she did not behave like a servant. She sat at the table with the others and her suggestion was bold and forward, not how one would expect a servant to talk or a grand lady for that matter.

Her accent when she spoke was on a par with the Earl and his Countess, not the accents of a servant or anyone else he could think of. She did not speak like him and his friends; she spoke like Julia, who had been given the best education money could buy while growing up.

He was at a loss as to what the woman's place was in the order of things and His Lordship certainly seemed shocked by her words, or perhaps it was just the outspoken way she voiced them.

He sent Simon off to Emily, where she was busy hanging washing on the line to dry. He had spoken of Julia's death before the child and he was afraid of what else he might say without thinking. He could only hope nobody told him what a martyr was before Charles was ready to tell him himself.

While he leaned on the rail and watched Julia's son busily trying to help Emily, he thought about Frances' words. He had no idea if she meant them, but she reminded him so much of Julia. She always saw the practical side of things first.

He had never considered marrying. Julia had been the love of his life and always would be, but Frances also had children and perhaps their father had been the love of her life.

He turned as she came to stand beside him, that mischievous little grin bringing a smile to his lips again.

"Forgive me, Sir," she said. "I had no right to embarrass you as I did. I am afraid living in the Americas did nothing for my social manners."

"You lived in the New World?"

"Yes."

"Tell me who you are, please. I took you for a servant, but now I am not so sure."

She laughed delightedly.

"I used to be Lady Frances Morgan and I was raised to be the wife of an important nobleman. I was betrothed to Lord Kennington when I was but ten years old and sent to live with his family."

Charles glanced at the house.

"That Lord Kennington?" He asked.

"Yes, that Lord Kennington. Adrian."

"What happened?"

"I fell in love with his brother."

Charles could only stare. His life was completely different, the principles of his class in no way resembling those of the nobility, but even a farmer could understand how disruptive it would be for a man to have his betrothed fall for his brother.

"And His Lordship forgave you?" He asked hesitantly.

"Mark persuaded Adrian to release me from my promise to him and we eloped; we ran away to the New World, found some land and built a small farm. We had two wonderful children; they were the happiest years of my life."

"And your husband? He is dead?"

Frances caught back a sob.

"He was killed in an Indian raid so I sold everything and brought the children back to England. Adrian and Elizabeth were kind enough to take us in and we have lived with them ever since."

"Then you, too, are of the nobility. You must marry within your own class."

Frances shook her head and her blonde waves shone in the sunlight making his heart skip as it never had since he lost Julia. Was there something about him which made him keep falling for ladies of quality?

"I have no idea what that is, Mr Carlisle. Because of the betrothal to Adrian, I am guilty of adultery; because that adultery was with his brother, I am guilty of incest. I will never be accepted and I do not want to be. Apart from Adrian and Elizabeth, who have been so good to me, those people are false. I would laugh at them all were it not for my children. Perhaps I deserve to be shunned; they do not."

Charles watched her carefully for a few moments, his thoughts taking him to a future he might share with this woman. He did not know her, not at all, but neither had he known Julia when she rode in on Guinevere and stole his heart. But despite the title, Julia was not of the nobility. Could he believe this lady could ever replace her? Did he want her to?

"The life of a farmer's wife is a hard one," he remarked.

"I know that; it is not new to me. At least here I will not have savage natives attacking and trying to kill me. We have had enough of that with the bishops these five years." Frances looked up at him and smiled. "I meant what I said, Sir. We could build a life together. Elizabeth wants me to have Sinclair Manor but she does not want to turn you out, or all your people here, and neither do I. It is a perfect solution and if you refuse, I shall have to return to Kennington Hall and live in a sort of limbo of not belonging anywhere with a dowager who hates me."

"Is that the alternative? Well, I suppose I am preferable to the Dowager."

They laughed together at his joke and it was somehow comfortable, as though they had known each other for years. He seemed just what Frances had been waiting for. He could never replace Mark, but that did not mean she could not learn to love him.

"Tell me about your wife," she said.

"Julia came here to escape a violent husband," he began. "We called each other husband and wife, but it was never blessed by any church, only by our love for one another."

Frances caught her breath.

"I am sorry," she said. "I just assumed…"

"It is a long story and I will tell you one day, but not today. Simon is not my natural son, but I love him dearly and you are right; he does need a mother."

"Can I return in a few days with my children," Frances asked. "I have a son and daughter; he is Mark, after his father, and she is

Katie. They are a little older than Simon, but will make him a fine brother and sister."

"I would like that."

***

On their arrival at Kennington Hall, Frances had her boxes and those of the children packed and prepared for the return journey to Suffolk the following day. Adrian had spent all morning trying to persuade her to give the plan more thought, but she would have none of it.

"Adrian, please stop nagging," she said. "This is fate, do you not see?"

He was concerned for her wellbeing but he had to admit to a certain degree of snobbery about his insistence that this plan was not a good one. Charles Carlisle might have been a hero to the Protestant cause, and he might, for some mysterious reason, be raising the son of Lord Summerville, but he was still a farmer.

It seemed odd to him that Frances was happy to accept such a life; he had never seen her on the farm in the Americas, never seen her life with Mark. In his mind she was still little Lady Frances, that shy, well brought up young lady who would one day be his countess.

She wore a little smile on her pretty face and a sparkle of excitement in her blue eyes which had not been there since the night he agreed to release her to his brother. She had looked happy then and she looked happy now.

"So you believe you can find a place with Charles Carlisle?" Adrian said, his arm sliding around her shoulders. "You believe you can make it work, that he will look after you?"

"I do. At least I am willing to find out. I would like your blessing, though."

He kissed her cheek.

"You have it. Just remember you always have a home here, you and the children no matter what. You do not have to stay if things do not work out."

***

She had no idea what living arrangements Charles had arranged for them until she arrived. He might think it was in order for her to move into the manor house with him, but that was one little nicety she had not yet relinquished. When she arrived, she was pleased to find he had prepared one of the cottages for himself and arranged for her and her children to have the manor house.

Charles waited in the courtyard as her coach rumbled across the stone ground and the children looked out excitedly at the farm. She had tried to explain to them what it would be like, but they had little memory of their own farm across the ocean and it was all an exciting novelty to them.

Simon greeted them with a smile of pleasure and Frances realised there were no other children here. This new brother and sister would likely be the first playmates the child had ever had and as they jumped down they all ran off towards the fields together. She turned to Charles expectantly. He was a fine looking man and he had a lovely smile, a smile which made her heart skip as it had not done since she lost Mark.

He stood with his hand out waiting to take hers. She caught hold of his hand and noticed how warm and comforting it felt. Then he took her by surprise as he pulled her to him and kissed her.

"We will be happy together," he said softly. "I feel it."

"I, too, feel it. I think we have Mark's blessing. Do you think we have Julia's?"

***

The marriage ceremony was the Protestant one Queen Elizabeth had restored, Cranmer's service in English. Frances recalled saying these same words to Mark in a small, hastily built wooden church on the other side of the world, but for Charles this was the first time. He and

Julia had made their own, private vows and kept them.

Adrian was there to give her away and Elizabeth attended her; she wanted to provide Frances with her own wedding gown for the occasion, but she refused.

"It is gorgeous, Elizabeth. It is very much like the one which was made for my wedding to Adrian, the one I never wore, and I do thank you, but no. I am going to be a farmer's wife again, and a farmer's bride would not wear a garment like this." She fingered the material for a moment, then smiled contentedly. "I have no need of fine fabrics," she went on. "Charles will feel uncomfortable if I wear this; it will remind him of just who I am and I do not want that. I do not want to be reminded of it myself either."

When Adrian led her into that church, he could not help but remember his own betrothal to her, to think what might have been. Would they have been happy together? Frances once said they would have, but the bliss they had each found with the two people who loved them would have escaped them altogether.

Now he could only hope and pray she could find the same happiness and bliss with this farmer as she had with Adrian's brother.

It was a strange sort of ceremony, not what the Earl and Countess were accustomed to at all, but there was no unnecessary formality and everyone seemed to be enjoying themselves.

Adrian almost envied them the freedom they would have and he understood at last how Frances could be happy with this life, why she preferred not to try to re-enter the society which shunned her.

While she was hugging Elizabeth, Adrian took the opportunity to speak to Charles.

"You will look after her?" He said. "I am trusting you."

Charles grinned.

"Frances is trusting me," he replied. "And that is far more important to me."

Adrian was longing to ease his curiosity and ask this man why he was raising Richard Summerville's son, but he did not quite have the courage. He could be wrong, after all; it could be just a coincidence that the boy so resembled him and if that were case, Mr Carlisle would take offence and quite rightly, too.

But he could not forget Richard's words when he asked him to keep an eye on Charles: *it is imperative he is kept safe. I have my reasons.*

There was dancing in the courtyard, strange instruments and jolly music played by Jacob's sons, and all three children went home with Jacob for the night. When everyone had gone, the newly wedded couple retreated to the house and sat on the settle together.

It was a peculiar atmosphere. These two hardly knew each other and to Frances that was nothing unusual; it was the normal thing among the aristocracy, but to Charles it was very strange and rather uncomfortable.

He took her hand hesitantly.

"Frances," he said. "You have done me a great honour by agreeing to marry me. I hope I can make you happy; I will do my best."

"And I will do my best to make you happy, Charles. You have given me something special by taking me as your wife. You have given me a place, a place for me and my children and for that I will always thank you."

They sat and talked for hours, not what either of them expected of their wedding night but somehow it came naturally. She told him all about Mark, how they had run away together, how they had built the farm together, and he told her about Julia.

"It is hard for you to talk about her, I can see," Frances said.

"It is still very raw. She suffered a horrendous and painful death and I shall always blame myself. Had I not been wounded she would never have been there."

"She would not want you to blame yourself."

"But I do, and I do not feel entitled to be happy."

"But you are?"

He nodded.

"I think I could love you, Frances. Do you think you could love me?"

"I think I already do."

He kissed her then, kissed her as he had once kissed Julia, stirred for her as he had once stirred for Julia and he could almost hear her soft, sweet voice telling him to be happy for all of them, for himself and his new wife and for their lost loves.

THE END

Book One – The Judas Pledge

Book Two – The Flawed Mistress

Book Three – The Viscount's Birthright

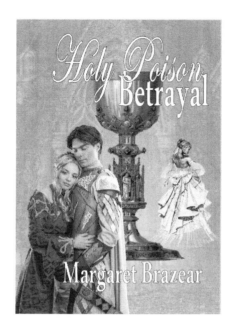

Book Four – Betrayal

Visit my website http://www.historical-romance.com for more about my other books.

The Romany Princess
Mirielle
The Scent of Roses
To Catch a Demon (free if you subscribe to my newsletter)
The Wronged Wife (Currently free to download)
A Man in Mourning
The Adulteress
The Crusader's Widow

The first chapters of all my books can be read at http://historical-fiction-on-kindle.blogspot.co.uk

Printed in Great Britain
by Amazon.co.uk, Ltd.,
Marston Gate.